Dallas Stories

Southwest Life and Letters

A series designed to publish outstanding new fiction and nonfiction about Texas and the American Southwest and to present classic works of the region in handsome new editions.

General Editors: Tom Pilkington, Tarleton State University; Suzanne Comer, Southern Methodist University Press.

Dallas Stories

By Marshall Terry

SOUTHERN METHODIST UNIVERSITY PRESS

First edition, 1987
Requests for permission to reproduce material from this work should be sent to:
Permissions
Southern Methodist University Press
Box 415
Dallas, Texas 75275

Library of Congress Cataloging-in-Publication Data

Terry, Marshall, 1931–
    Dallas stories.

ᴺᴵᶠ   (Southwest life & letters)
    1. Dallas (Tex.)—Fiction. I. Title.
II. Series.
PS3570.E699D3   1987   813'.54   87-9755
ISBN 0-87074-254-X
ISBN 0-87074-255-8 (pbk.)

"Grass," "The Antichrist," "Endzone," and "The Real" appeared originally in
Southwest Review; "The Silvering of Trees" and "Whatever Happened to Danny
McBride?" in *Vision;* "Another Dimension" in *D Magazine;* "Poet" in *New and
Experimental Literature* (Texas Center for Writers Press, 1975); and "Gretta,
Claude, and Sally" in *The Bicentennial Collection of Texas Short Stories* (Texas Cen-
ter for Writers Press, 1974).

Designed by Whitehead & Whitehead

Illustration by Wanda Gamble

To
Toni, Toinette, and Mary
and to the memory of
Margaret L. Hartley

Contents

Preface

THESE stories are collected from a group written over the past twenty years. I hope they reflect the dynamism of a fascinating city with its own distinctive myth and metaphor over that period. Yet, like Joyce's *Dubliners,* they are meant to be stories of the spirit as well as of the social scene. For example, the one not physically set in Dallas seems to me to define a certain need and striving of the place as well as any.

Are these characters "real"? No, not drawn from actual models, or from TV either.

Dallas Stories is dedicated to my family and to Margaret L. Hartley, who served the *Southwest Review* in various capacities for thirty-five years and was acknowledged to have discovered and encouraged more writers in the Southwest than any other editor during that time. She was a stalwart person, from whom I and others in Texas and beyond learned lessons of integrity, grace, and courage.

I am indebted to Southern Methodist University for its encouragement to its faculty through the years to freely think, teach, and write, and I am grateful to my publisher, Keith Gregory, and my editor, Suzanne Comer, for their faith in these stories.

Marshall Terry
Dallas Hall
Dallas

Dallas Stories

The Prince of Dallas

BEN RAY CLARK stood in his office at the top of the Texas Drilling Tower and looked out over the view he had of other high, metal-plated buildings rising above the downtown area and beyond, over the rich, stretching prairie. Often he could see nearly as far as Fort Worth, and he could see the complex of industrial districts and the white cotton on the black earth between the two cities. As he stood there, so high above it all, he was thinking of the Myth of Dallas: not the old Neely Bryan bit exactly, for he knew just how corny that was, but the idea of the lack of strong geographical or other reasons for a great city to have sprung up, to have been built here, by strong men, by pirates and pioneers. They were all proud of that, and it had, he thought, its degree of truth. It used to be he could feel the thrill of that—usually looking out from Fanch's office so much the same as this one he himself had come to—and be moved by the sustaining myth of the city that now was his. But today he was troubled, and he turned from the stretch of glass and stood on the dull carpet with his hand on the beautiful wood of his desk and let his gaze go around this office. It was still strange to him that he had come to have his being in this place.

Except in its height and luxury the office was really not so much like Fanch's. Old Fanch had no books at all, whereas Ben Ray Clark had a number of first editions—poetry and

1

history mostly—on the shelves he'd commanded built along one wall. (He was known for his promotion of cultural institutions in the city, and Cissy was often photographed now as one of the city's queens of culture.) Nor did Fanch have paintings on his walls, these really rather sorry originals of local talent which somehow Clark felt should be encouraged. He walked across the room and beheld, as he did each day, the fine craggy features of his man, his poet Frost, hunched with white hair blowing and scarf loose around his old neck reading—or saying—"The Gift Outright" at the Inauguration. He loved the picture, and the poem. It was set on the wall by some of his civic plaques, just next to the Salesmanship Award.

He thought of how singular a juxtaposition that was, and of how strange the route was that had brought him here to behold them both, both his, on this wall.

He'd had this office now for a few months more than a year. He'd been by several years, at thirty-four, the youngest chief executive of a major Dallas company when he was named president of Texas Drilling Corporation, replacing Fanch. Henry had been good about it, hard as it was for the old boy; he was still chairman, but he'd let young Clark run the show. (Except, of course, for his invaluable and constant advice and counsel, and the endless monologues in executive committee meetings each Wednesday morning, a habit after so many years too hard to break and which had to be indulged. All in all he and Fanch got along well, as it had to be, for his own sake as well as for TexDrill—and Dallas.) But the fine craggy face of Robert Frost peering at him from over spectacles on his wall did not help steer him from his troubled thoughts of this morning. For it was a big day for Big D, a hell of a big day for Dallas, as Fanch had told them all a thousand times by now.

He went and sat at his lovely desk, which was absolutely clear save for the onyx-eye paperweight set squarely in the middle of its sheen and depth, and folded his hands and waited for it to be time to go. He had not liked that ad in the morning's paper; they should not have run that ad, someone was asleep at the switch down there. But it was done, and there was nothing to do but pray that the day would go well. It had started well. He'd come in here and watched, as Cissy slept at home, the program on his wall TV. It had gone well in Fort Worth, and very well then a short while ago at Love. He had not liked the warrant for making citizens' arrests, but everyone was edgy. It was the stupid incident involving Stevenson that got them worried. But Clark was sure it would be all right. He had grown to be much less sensitive and "fuzzy" (as Fanch said) in his thinking in the last few years, and now he knew that there was nothing personal in all this no matter what anybody thought or how anybody felt. It could not be personal; all that was irrelevant. It was political, and they all knew it and knew how to play it. It was strictly political and practical, on all sides. What it meant was an airport and a federal center—it had damn well *better* mean that to us, as his beloved "Uncle Henry" had said.

He sat and considered that, no matter what you thought, the guy had it, he really had it. My God, what style. And he thought how lovely she had looked over there in Cowtown, on the screen. Thinking of that, he thought of Cissy lying there all creamed and curled up asleep at the same hour, and wondered if she had dragged up out of bed yet. Yes, she would be up by now, and he should call her. She had bridge this afternoon. All this meant nothing to dear, dear Cissy; she was really quite oblivious. Nearly everyone was. Including, he thought, with a sudden twinge of some irra-

3

tional bitter feeling, Ben Ray Clark, who had, in another
time and life, as he now dimly remembered, presumed to
desire to be a poet.

It was about time to go. Neither he nor Fanch was on the
welcoming committee, but Fanch and his wife Emmalou
were to be at a subhead table for the luncheon. He buzzed
Miss Hopkins and told her she could signal down to have
the car ready. Then he stood and was still standing vacantly
by the desk when Fanch burst in. He'd thought the old man
would have busted his britches to get on down there by now.

"Well, you ready, boy?" Fanch said. "Ready for the big
day? You see it on the television? Son of a bitch wouldn't
wear that hat, would he?"

"I understand he doesn't like hats, of any kind," Clark said.

"Yeah, but for Christ's sake, 'when in Rome,' eh? We got
to get going. You sure you don't want to ride over with me
and Walter? Say, Walter just told me this, tickled hell out of
me. You hear it? They were up there, getting ready to come
down to wild and woolly Texas, you see, and he's trying to
tell her just how to do, just exactly how to act, you know.
And he's worried about her a little, you see, mixing in with
all these horny Texans and he tells her to be goddamn careful and not let herself get caught alone with any of 'em,
they're not past trying a little hanky-panky even with the
likes of her. So when he tells her that she just smiles at him
sweetly and says, 'Thanks for the advice, Jack, but I think
you better watch out for yourself. From what I hear, it's not
my ass they're after!'"

Fanch laughed his belly laugh that could be heard throughout a crowded room and ended with piglike snorts and
giggles.

The younger man did not acknowledge the joke, or the
fact that it shocked him deeply. In a moment he said, sternly,
in the manner and voice that had earned him consistently

4

through his life the respect of older men: "No, I'll take my car. I may not come straight back here."

"Okay," said Henry Fanch. "See you there. We'll wave at you from below the throne, eh?"

After Fanch left, Ben Ray Clark stood another minute or so alone in his office. He did not mind cigars, and smoked a Gold Label himself every so often. But Fanch was of the old guard rough-and-tough dime cigar school, and the smoke from this weed, along with his foul and tasteless joke, seemed unendurable just now, made the whole office seem to stink. Ben Ray Clark captured a mental image of himself and adjusted the vest of his narrow dull suit, preparing to go out by Miss Hopkins and take his car along the streets of his crowded city. He had begun to wear these suits with vest and to wear his Phi Beta Kappa key on a thin gold chain at the vest several years ago, even before he had changed his colorless rims for a pair of mottled horn-rimmed glasses. These made him look older.

Then, as ready as he could make himself, he walked out of his office and took the elevator down to his car in the parking garage, to drive himself to the luncheon at the Trade Mart.

2

WHEN old Pete Elliott called me down here from up in Dallas I was surprised. It had been a long time since the sorry devil had bothered to be in touch, despite all his annual Christmas card words about our beautiful "eternal friendship" and all. I'd been out seeing over the place here, and down in Mexico, in the plane and riding sore-assed in that damn jeep for more than a month, and I was tired, and not in sorts, not even quite the amiable, lovable bastard that

5

I usually am. "Redwine?" he says. "Where have you been? I've called about a hundred times."

"Well, I do have a few little things to tend to," I said. "Not real big deals like you Dallas boys, but a few animals that do need looking after. What's on your mind, Brother Elliott?"

"How's your mother?" he says. "And Aglaia—how's Aglaia? And Uncle Sweet? You had any rain down there?"

So then I knew something was up. Any idiot could figure it. Old Pete Elliott, as far as I'd ever been able to see, didn't give a left-handed crap about his *own* dear mama, let alone mine. And he'd never met Uncle Sweet, who stays in Mexico, but once, and Aglaia could never stand him since he got so bombed that time and tried to make out with her in the swimming pool and she like to had to drown him. Aglaia always kind of liked Ben Ray, but Pete Elliott, she always said, was too much on the make for everything and he always made her feel itchy.

"Fine, fine," I said. "Nice of you to ask."

"Anything going on down there?" he says.

"Going on? What in hell you mean, *going on?* What's up, Peter?"

"Well—" Then I could tell it was really something important to him, or to whoever was involved, since I'd never seen Pete Elliott acting really on his own in anything yet. It was something important, I could tell, because he didn't want me to think it was.

"Nothing special," he says. "I was just wondering if old Ben had drifted down your way. I've been trying to get in touch with him and—and I wondered if he might be visiting you. You know how close they are at his place, and this is— It's a business deal, actually. Have you seen Ben Ray?"

"No," I said. "We haven't seen Ben Ray for two–three

years. Since he was crowned, anyway. What's wrong? Is he a damn missing person or something?"

"Oh, no. Nothing like that. I'm sure someone up here knows where he is, if I can get the idiots to tell me. And it's nothing important, really. Well, it was good to talk to my old compadre anyway. When are you going to grace us with one of your rare visits?"

"Not soon," I said. "You heard of many people heading your way lately? I was there last November, me and Leroy—"

"Well, why didn't you—? Oh. Well, you know that folks here are still in shock over that thing that happened, and all the rest of it. You should have been here, Redwine, the last month or two. It's been rough. What a damn fool thing to have a whole city branded with by some nut! You know Dallas, Redwine, it's not like that. It's not like they're all saying and writing now. But we'll pull out of it, old buddy."

"That's right," I said. "Sorry I can't help you, Pete. Well, whoever you're charging this to, amigo, it's costing them a fortune. Hope you find Ben Ray. Say, you asked Cissy?"

"Yeah," Pete Elliott said. "I should have thought of that. Goodbye, Redwine."

He'd thought of that all right, and if Ben Clark's own wife didn't know where he was, that was something else, all right. It sounded like Ben Ray had skipped out or something. But he hadn't been here to the ranch for several years and then just that one time. He'd enjoyed it though, mostly just riding out by himself alone, until I had Osmenio trail him along so the damn fool wouldn't get lost or get his head split open by some surprised cedar cutter.

I'd always liked Ben Ray Clark. We were all in school together, up there at Liberty College where my family made me go because it was in the family to go there, and after

7

sophomore year Peter Elliott and Ben Clark and me were pretty close in the fraternity and Ben Ray and I roomed together one year. They were both from around up there in Pennsylvania and then we graduated and both of them wanted to write—you know, all those English majors had a novel in a drawer up there, and so did Ben and Elliott—but didn't know what to do in the meantime, so I got Clark to come on down here and he went into the geology program with me at the University. I just goofed it, thinking a little oil and water geology wouldn't hurt me in running things here, and Uncle Sweet thought it was a good idea, and it has been. But Ben Clark got hot at it, though I expect it never did thrill him too much, and he came out of it in just three years with a Ph.D. in geology. Then he went to Dallas with a company, and later Pete Elliott came sneaking on down and joined him there. Well, he's—I mean Pete is—about where he should be now, I expect, doing p.r. work for an electronics outfit, but Ben Ray Clark . . . ? I don't know, Aglaia and I have often wondered about old Ben Ray. You take a quick look at it and you'd have to say he's done well, real well.

But it generally had seemed to me that Pete Elliott was always so damn ready to get sucked up in it, not that he was a bad sort of kid or anything, but that Ben Clark was just not like that. Which was why I always liked Ben more, I guess. I guess the thing is that they both got sucked up in it, and like Aglaia says, who in the hell am I to be the one to say anything about that? Like, I've always had a lot of regard for Dallas and folks there, and then I happened to be up there, you know, when it happened. And I remember that Leroy and me just looked at each other, early in that afternoon, and he said, "Let's get the hell out of here, Redwine," and we did.

But Elliott and Clark, now, they're there, and I supposed they'd work it out all right there. They'd have to.

I wondered where Ben Ray Clark was, but decided not to mention it to Aglaia or anybody. I expected they'd find him soon enough. And it set me to thinking about the old days in college at Liberty and about how close we all were for a few years there. It's strange, you know, having friends, and how quick you lose them when you have to get out and get to doing what you have to do in the world.

3

"WHERE in the hell is Ben Ray Clark?"

The old boy had come raging into my office like a stuck pig. I hardly knew him, except as we all knew the name of Henry W. Fanch. It was a very big name in Dallas, an old one, and Henry W. was actually one of the few men who had started as oil wildcatters and had built companies who bothered to get involved in the civic affairs of Dallas. The others in the big oil crowd mostly let it all rock by.

Fanch glared at me. He was a hard little man with jowls and pinpoint eyes like hard blue onions. We had been with the Fanches at Ben Ray Clark's on several different evenings, but then so had fifty others. He slammed his cigar out in my desk ashtray; it sat there stinking beneath my nose.

"I don't know," I said. "Maybe he's off somewhere getting some rest. He probably needs it. Just where, I couldn't say. We haven't been as close as we used to be."

I knew that Ben Ray was gone, and that they were worried. I'd had a call from Cissy, his pale anemic wife.

"Well, he's been gone," Fanch said, "no trace, two weeks. He's got to get back here and head the goddamn hospital drive. We can hush it up, that he's gone and we don't know where, for a while, but— You're his goddamn friend, Elliott. We want you to find him."

He took out another cigar, unwrapped it, and licked it ready. Suddenly I felt more or less sorry for the old man. All of them had taken it hard; and taken it, and taken it. The press, all over the world, would not let up. They wanted a victim, and without Oswald, it was Dallas. Now his "dear boy" Ben Ray was gone, just vanished, and I felt sorry for Fanch. He suddenly looked more than his seventy years, and tired.

He spoke, very gently, to me: "Pete—that's your name, isn't it? We'd all consider this a very big favor. You'd be doing me, and TexDrill, a service. And his family. And Dallas, boy, and Dallas. That hospital drive has got to go, not only because of my personal involvement in it, you understand. It's got to go for *Dallas*. And he's chairman of the drive, and we kick off in a week. A *week*. Why would the boy run out like this, not leave a word to anyone? Hell, I don't care if he goes to the moon, but not like this. I tell you Cissy is worried sick. She's called off all her bridge, and she's stopped her League work. But we don't want the authorities in—not yet. If he's dead, he's dead, it's no kidnap obviously. So— You know him, where he'd be. Didn't you grow up together? You go find him. Do anything you need, boy. We can't put a goddamn stuffed dummy up there next week, Elliott, and expect the goddamn dummy to run the drive."

"Yes, sir. The only thing, I was due to go to Australia in three days to—" I was going to promote a new transistor line and had been looking forward to the trip tremendously.

"Shit," said Henry W. Fanch. "A goddamn kangaroo could do that. I talked to Luther. He said for you to go do this."

Now he was not being so gentle, and I was losing my sense of sympathy for him.

"Listen to me, Elliott," he said harshly. "You go find that sonofabitchin' puppy. You hear?"

I heard. I walked over my cherished carpet and looked out at Dallas from my eighth-floor window. Most of it loomed over me, and looking up I saw the Dallas sky, that endless blue with the sun that looks twice as bright from behind air-conditioned steel, and I thought, God, if he's snapped the traces, he could be out in the world anywhere. I remembered he always did want to go to Spain and see the bullfights and fish in the mountain streams. He'd wanted me to go along and fish with him where Hemingway and his friend had fished. But that was years ago, before he was the boy-wonder president of the Texas Drilling Corporation. Now I hardly ever saw him, maybe once in a while for a drink at the City Club. But he had his time planned out to the minute now, and I didn't think anybody really knew Ben Ray Clark anymore, in his horn-rimmed glasses and the strict narrow suits and vests he always wore, never smiling, aloof, alone. He used to smile, some. Back then we called him Ben; *Ben Ray* he adopted after he came to Texas, though it was his real name. I think he thought it helped him in this double-naming state, and I think it did. I was sure I didn't know where the damn fool was.

When that absurdity, the assassination, happened, Ben Ray Clark was one of the most shook up around here that I saw, and there were plenty who were shook. He was one of about a dozen chosen to represent Dallas at one of the civic forums that took place. The point was to bear up under all the crazy pointing fingers and tell the world "what's *good* about Dallas." In his talk Ben Ray Clark said that he had freely chosen to come to Dallas to make a life for himself

11

and would do so now again, for nowhere else was there more opportunity to work hard and get ahead and cherish the old, true values. Of course, the little ass was the living prime example of that, which was why they had to have him up there. His talk was well received, and they had hoped that CBS might pick it up, but of course those bastards used a more critical one . . . But there was a funny thing about the speech. Jim Leary, TexDrill's p.r. man, told me about it. Jim advised Ben Ray to omit the words "our guilt and shame" which had been in his original draft, and then old Fanch got wind of it and made sure he did. Fanch was very pleased with the result, which got good local coverage, and I heard the old man at the club saying that it gave a good counterbalance to all the hysterical crap that was being said about our town. And so it did. I don't care what you think, you've got to admit this if you've got any sense at all: Dallas deserved some scorn and judgment, but not all that it got. Not by a million inches.

After that, a month or more after the assassination, a little after Christmas, Ben Ray and his wife had their annual egg-nog party for about three hundred people in their big pale house on Turtle Creek. And God, ye host did act more than a little grim. Several people noticed it. I went up, with a real drink that I'd cadged and another one for him—sometimes he'd walk off outside with me at those things and we'd have a talk. Like years before. But he said a few cool things to me, as if I were just another of these people he so obviously scorned in his damned superior way, instead of his oldest friend in town, and walked off, and went upstairs, and let poor Cissy have the party.

I hadn't seen him since, and now he was gone.

I made some phone calls in the city, discreet inquiries, not to alarm anybody, since I knew Fanch and TexDrill were fudging all over the place for Ben Ray, making it up that he was here or there, but running out of time. But I knew he wasn't in Dallas, and so I called around the country to some of our old buddies, to Charlie Tares in San Francisco and Louis O'Malley in New Orleans and even Bob Lee Bell in Vegas, though Ben Ray Clark never even played rummy for matchsticks in his life. They had no word. When I finally got through to our old compadre Redwine Walker playing Lord of Creation down on his ranch he was his usual helpful self. Either Ben Clark or I could have dropped dead without bothering him too very greatly.

I went over and lay on the couch and smoked. I tried to stop thinking of the boobs on Redwine Walker's sister Aglaia and to think of Ben. He never said much to me or anybody, and not just lately. That was why he was supposed to be so wise, because he was so quiet. But a hundred times, in college, it was me, Pete Elliott, who carried the half-ass around on my shoulders. If Ben Ray Clark thought he would ever have made the fraternity without Pete Elliott behind him, he was crazy. The damn guy, in those days, in the beginning, just hung around. We never expected him to contribute much, and he never did. A poor townie boy, from right near the college. I was from Philadelphia. Most folks low-rated Ben, which was easy to do, thought he was a zero, and most of the girls thought he was a bird. But he was a sensitive guy, and he could do poetry a thousand miles ahead of mine, and we were friends all that time without knowing each other very well, and had a real good time, before and after we let that Redwine Walker clown into the group. All the girls except Perkie, she'd always been in love with Ben.

Perkie. Where was she? Wasn't she in New York now, with a publishing house? Yes, Clark had said one time that she was there a year or two ago; had said that I should send my still unpublished, unfinished novel manuscript to her for criticism. Ben Clark could say cutting things like that; it was a side you had to remember, that he could be a bastard.

That was strange, that Perkie was in New York, because, lying here, inhaling deeply, coughing, I could remember suddenly so vividly—as the most vivid thing I could remember about him—the Thanksgiving holiday our first year at Liberty. We'd gone in to New York, his first time in the city. We stayed with a Jewish buddy in a skyscraper apartment near the Village and walked the streets at night. And Ben Ray got separated, and came in about 3 A.M. with some wild story about talking to a bum who claimed to be a painter and a cop had taken a crack at them with a nightstick in the park, and they'd run out, and the bum had shared some cheap wine with him and told him he knew Ben Ray must be a painter or some kind of artist too, because of the way he talked to him and listened to him. And Ben Ray tried to tell me about this bum's stories of Thomas Wolfe and Maxwell Bodenheim in the Village and how life was a delicate adventure and all that, and I tried to stay awake even though I thought he must be making most of it up to compensate for getting lost like a rube, and I fell asleep in the bed next to him. But, my God, that was ancient history, and Ben Ray had been to New York, in and out, hurrying from one building to another, like we all had, a hundred times since then.

Still, that stayed so strangely in my mind.

I got up and pressed the buzzer on my desk and told the girl to get me on the evening jet to New York. Then I called my wife.

"But Peter," she said, "you're going to be gone all the way across the world, to Australia, for so long, and I thought you'd be—"

"I'm sorry, baby. I don't even know if that's still on. I may end up in Spain or some damn place as it is on this. It's a civic thing, something I have to do. You know how that is."

14

"Yes," she said.

"I'll be back as soon as I can. I love you."

"All right," she said.

I took a suit and some shirts from the closet in the office and threw them in a bag and had our driver take me out to Love. Dallas looked golden in the dusk, great golden buildings sitting on the endless flat land. I really loved this country. On the jet I buckled in and we lifted off and then I got a drink and drank it with my eyes shut, happy in a way, grateful to Ben Ray Clark for this chance just to fly on out and go wherever he was and find him. I stayed up most of the night in the hotel, thinking and feeling foolish at being in New York, and in the morning I went to the apartment house near the Village where we had stayed on that Thanksgiving holiday more than fifteen years ago.

The Zuckers' apartment, decorated in white and gold, hadn't changed, and after Mrs. Zucker, startled but working hard at being pleased, had let me in and we were sitting in the living room, I remembered sitting in the same room, being polite, happy, and quite grown up, drinking Courvoisier and hacking on H. Upmann cigars on our first evening in the city. Mr. Zucker had worn a Liberty beanie and Sam Zucker, more Ben's friend than mine, had told us about the dates he'd lined up for us and all the sights we had to see. Now Mr. Zucker was dead, and Sam, a Harvard lawyer, was in a government agency in Washington. I'd liked Sam all right, but our views had never meshed, we had not been in touch for many years, and I felt very out of place now sitting here.

"So, are you running out of Dallas too?" she said. It startled me.

"Ma'am?"

"I mean, I can tell it must have been hard for people living there. Such a senseless thing. We thought of you boys being there. Sam was very much affected. He waited to come home, and then he went into his room, where you boys stayed, and cried. A grown man, but many people cried."

"Yes, ma'am. People wept in Dallas."

"I am sure. A senseless thing. It could have happened anywhere."

It was the damnedest thing. Sitting up here, talking to this little gentle lady, for the first time I really seriously wondered if that were so. Quickly I said, "Mrs. Zucker, have you by any chance seen, or heard from, Ben Ray Clark?"

"Bennie? No. But I remember Bennie so well. Sam Senior liked him so. He said you were a city boy, meant for the city, but Bennie, he thought Bennie was not a city boy and should stay out of it. No, I have not seen Bennie since that time—how many years ago? But Sam has a nice card from him, like from you, every year. I have not seen him since that time. Why? Is he missing?"

"Oh, no. He's temporarily out of touch with his firm. He's president of his company now, you know—one of the major oil drilling and supply companies in the world—and they need to get hold of him on some business. And I thought he might have—called."

She smiled.

"It's strange, that you should have thought that," she said.

"Yes," I said.

"Well, it's nice to see you again. And to hear of Bennie— of Ben—Clark. He was a nice boy. So shy. A president, so young? He is doing well."

"Real well. How's Sam liking the Washington whirl by now? I mean—"

"Sam believes in what he is doing," she said. "Sam is not rich, but he is happy."

"I'm sure," I said, and got on out of there.

On the sidewalk somehow the old magic of New York got to me, and I felt young again. It had been a long time, believe me, since I had felt young. Thinking of Ben, I turned right and walked on through the gates of Washington Square and into the park. For a while I had the most certain feeling that Ben Clark was here, and that if he was, he would be in the Village. But it was queer: I didn't remember it at all. In the daytime, except for Washington Square, and the narrow streets, and a little playhouse I passed, it didn't seem like the Village, or anyway like an eighteen-year-old kid had remembered it. I roamed around looking at everyone, and they stared back at me. I stopped, pretending to need a light, to ask the stairwell loungers if they knew him, had seen anyone like Ben Ray Clark. I was sure I'd turn a corner and see him, in vest and glasses, slim and silent, peering at the strange people, saying nothing. I felt him near somewhere, the silly son of a bitch.

And so I kept wandering all over the place, until I didn't even know if I was still in the Village or not, up and down the crummy streets, into queer joints and out of coffeehouses, by the sounds of high-pitched laughter and the strum of flamenco guitars, peering into tattered bookshops and curio shops, but there was no Ben Ray Clark. All the people seemed to sneer at me. Half-running finally, following a gang of six tough colored boys and a white girl in a sweatshirt and black leotards, I found myself back in the park. Then the gang stopped and one of the boys said something, and they all, the boys and the girl, made the ancient obscene gesture at me, laughing at me. Some of the checker players looked up from their stone boards and one of them, a very old dirty man, laughed too, and joined in giving me the finger. I stopped and stood where I was, stupidly, and then began to boil with anger and frustration. All at once I knew why their gestures came at me: it must have

17

been the small white Stetson that I wore. It took all the will I had not to rip it off and throw it away from me, or to stuff it up under my Alligator coat. It infuriated me. I did not wear it as a symbol; I would not have it taken for one. I wore it because I liked it. I wore it because I am, and have always been, romantic.

I walked away from them until I found a fairly nice-looking restaurant at the border of the Village. It had tables set outside, a mockery in the coldness, but like an idiot I felt like sitting there. Inside there was sawdust on the floor and a long crowded bar, laughing and talking, tables packed around, not well lit, and I squeezed in at the bar, wearing my hat, and got a double Scotch.

I was terribly tired. My eyes wandered over the room. I could not think why I was in the place, and the whole quest, or whatever it was, seemed absurd. Then I lifted the glass and saw Ben Ray Clark sitting at a table where the room broke into another room. He was sitting facing half away from me talking to a girl, a girl with a high-pinned mane of hair. She was a beautiful girl. I pushed away from the bar and walked towards the table.

The man looked up. He was a slight, delicate-featured man, but not Ben Clark. He looked at me. The girl looked up too, stopping their conversation. She was a very light-skinned Negro girl.

"What is it, cowboy?" she said, kindly.

When I got back to the bar of my hotel I drank, of all the stupid things, a Manhattan. I felt a fool. I was sure Ben Ray was in Spain, or Africa, or on the moon, and I was pissing time out the window and had best go home, notwithstanding Fanch, or Fanch plus Dallas, hospital, and all, and get ready to escape Down Under. In the middle of the sweetly gagging Manhattan I remembered Perkie Adamson.

Oh well, I thought. As long as you're here, play it out. I

18

looked up the number of the publishing house in the directory and asked for her.

"Miss Adamson is out today," a rasping voice said. "She's sick at home."

I took a cab to her place. It was an apartment on Riverside Drive, by Columbia. It was an old stone place, and I worked an elevator up to the third floor and walked down a rotten hallway and peered in the dark to find the letter on her door. I knocked.

Perkie opened the door.

"Good Christ," she said. "Pete Elliott. Come in, Pete."

She led me up a little entrance hall. Back down the hall were other rooms, and I looked over my shoulder that way as I followed her in. She pointed to a chair in a parlor, where I sat.

"Well, Peter," she said.

I did not know what to say. I stared at her. My being with her was unreal.

"I understand you're not feeling well."

Perkie Adamson looked terrible.

Her yellow hair had gotten dark and snarly, and she wore large glasses over the blue eyes that used to sparkle and tease the Liberty boys. From reading so many sorry first novels, I thought. She had on a terrycloth robe and slippers, and her nose was red and scaly under the nostrils. I saw that she really was sick and that it would have surprised hell out of her to ask if she had heard from Ben Ray Clark.

She asked me if I'd like a drink and I said, just to build some kind of a bridge, sure. She brought me a tap-water bourbon.

"You look great," I said. "It's been a long time, Perkie."

"Tell me things," she said. "I never hear. That all seems another world and time. Since Daddy died, I never even hear anything from the college. Tell me about you, Pete.

19

How many brats do you have by now?"

"None. You never married, did you, Perkie?"

That was a beautiful thing to say.

"No. I only had one love in my life, you know. Oh, don't worry, not you, boy. Although we had our moments, didn't we? You even asked me to marry you once, do you remember? When you were loaded. One of those rare times. And I stole your pin and wore it on my bra. But you said you didn't remember and raised holy hell about the pin. Do you recall that? Not that it matters. But that was a lot of fun, in those days, wasn't it, Peter? Oh, how's that drink?"

"Fine, Perkie. It really is good to see you."

She was sitting across from me on a couch, her knees coming through the robe. They were good knees, she still had good legs. But her mouth had gone slack and ugly. It struck me that Perkie was old—middle-aged. She reached in her robe pocket for a used Kleenex and blew her nose, then kept dabbing at it.

We had all known Perkie there at Liberty. All the boys had. Her poor father for about a hundred years was the head of the maintenance staff. The love of her life, of course, was Ben Clark. He treated her beautifully, and they read poetry together. In a way, a very corny way, you might say Ben kind of redeemed her soul. He insisted she go on to college, which she did, and I suspected he'd helped her along since. I had always thought that if the little ass had had more guts he might even have married the girl.

"Why did you come to see me, Pete?"

"For old times' sake. I had a minute, remembered you were—"

She was laughing. I was tired of being laughed at today, but didn't blame her. She was right. It was pretty bad. I started to smile back at her, but then she came cutting in:

"Sweet Pete, the old word king. How much do you get by the word now, Pete?"

"All right," I said, and stood up and put the drink down.

She snuffled into the Kleenex. For a second I thought she was going to get up too. But she leaned forward and grinned at me.

"He called me, Pete. I know where the lost boy is."

So. Sweet Lord.

"Okay, Perkie. Where?"

"We had a good talk. He always calls me. I've not actually seen him, you know, for years. But we talked. You know where, Pete. You would know if you'd just think a minute. Where else would it be?"

"He doesn't have anyone up there."

"No. But it's the place. You know."

And I did, of course. Suddenly I knew too that I should have known before, because after all we were all young and happy and free together there at the college. It was where Ben became somebody. And also I realized that it had been me, not him, I had been searching for here in the city. Ben Ray would never have gone back to the Village. No, it was Pete Elliott who would do that, if he could leave the hat behind. I began to laugh, softly.

"It's weird, isn't it?" Perkie said.

"Yes, baby. It's damn weird. Strange. Did he say anything special?"

"No. Just talked. Oh, he said some Dallas bloodhound would be along, probably you, and to tell you to go to hell if you did come by."

Perkie leaned back on the couch to arrange her robe, which had fallen slightly open.

"I always liked you fairly well, Pete," she said, "given what an ass you are. But Ben, you see—or do you?—was al-

21

ways a gentleman. He was what none of the rest of you were, or understood in the least. He was naturally a gentleman."

I just left then. There was no reason to say anything, to stay longer.

Yet, to be honest, strangely wrought up as I was, I will always wonder if I would have left so quickly if Perkie's face had not been splotched and swollen, her nose not so red and raw.

On the plane to Pittsburgh, sipping at an ice-bound Scotch and smoking a cigarette, I thought about Perkie and the college days. I understood that the Surgeon General was coming out with a report blasting the weeds and I thought I would try to give them up. In Pittsburgh I rented a car, decided not to check in with Fanch yet, and started for the college. As I drove, snow was in cold patches by the road, and then deeper reservoirs of snow appeared beside me. I arrived at Liberty, driving down the five miles of bad road from the town to the college, in the evening just at dark. The campus looked beautiful, white and pure, under the smooth, piled-up snow.

I went up the steps of the ugly old dormitory where we had all lived (including Perkie, half the time) and went then downstairs into the old fraternity parlor, and there was Ben Ray Clark. Dressed in cords and a turtleneck sweater pulled on inside out, sitting on the same old sagging couch with his feet, in the range boots Redwine had equipped him with, thrust up on a table. He had a writing board up in front of him and was staring at a fire of red- and blue-burning logs.

"Hello, Pete," he said.

I sat down by him and watched the fire.

"You have some people worried," I said.

He laughed. "How's Fanch?" he said.

"Cissy has been worried sick."

"Oh hell. I talked to Cissy. She knows where I am. I told her not to tell anyone, especially you. You want a belt?"

He lifted a jug of something from the pocked floor. I shook my head, but then, as he held it there, took a long swallow. It was rye.

"Jesus," I said. "Well, are you about ready to come back?"

"Not going back," said Ben Ray Clark.

"I see. What are you going to do?"

"Stay here. Teach maybe. I talked to old Dean Mueller, remember him? Maybe if I endow myself a chair they'll let me teach. I have all the requisite degrees, you know."

"Oh yes, buddy, I do know." I reached down and hauled up the rye. "So that's it? Just cut out on everything and teach? Rocks and all that bit? That's what you're going to do?"

"No. Poetry. I'm going to do poetry. Here, want to see it—the first of it? My great work. Don't know what to call it—'The King Is Dead—Long Live—Our City!'"

He had to be a little crocked by now, sitting here with that jug, but not that much. The poem, handwritten on a pad he handed me from the board, was a very sober poem. Really very sober. It had been done at different times, with ballpoint, then black ink, and ballpoint again.

"Read it," he said. "You may read it, dear old friend and p.r. wizard. I would appreciate your comments. It has to do with your game: image."

Settling back, turning away from him, I looked at it. It began, "He took a twelve-dollar gun . . ."

I read it through. It ended: "Oh God / It happened here." I sank back and stared into the fire.

"I think it's terrible," I said slowly, then, trying to say true and to speak out of whatever feeling I'd had for him all the way back, all the way back to here, where we were, so

23

strangely, now. "And incredible. For you to have written this. And Ben, I think that you should burn it. Burn it right now in this fire and forget it. And come home. If you burn this now, then you can come back home."

He said nothing, not a word.

"My God," I said, "if anyone ever saw this crazy sophomoric poem, you'd be—"

"An enemy of the people?"

"Don't be so stupidly romantic! Aren't there enough idiots playing that role now? Do you want to join them all in a little private Walden? Maybe we could get Fanch to build it for you—you could live in a wing of his damn hospital. That would be as good as staying here, wouldn't it?"

"Sure," he said. "What the hell. Just go home."

"That's right. This for sure isn't your goddamn home. You live in Dallas, boy. Like I do . . ."

My God, I sounded to myself just like Fanch.

Ben Ray Clark laughed, laughed at me, the bastard. And it was just then that I realized how much I hated him.

I got up out of that trap of a chair.

"Well," I said, "are you coming back?"

"I don't know."

"What shall I—?"

"Tell him anything you want to. Anything you need to. I'm sorry, Pete. Sorry they sent you, I mean. Goddamn everything. It's been a long time since we were here, hasn't it, Pete? A long time."

Yes, I said to myself, hating him, and thought how young he looked, how unchanged from that time, so young and slim and pure. But he was not pure, the fool with his pious poetic blasphemies about our city. He was a dipped stick, like me.

I walked out. I took the poem, why exactly I can't say. I had to have it. He let me go out with it, didn't call me back. I hope he understood. That I just wanted it, had to have it. I hope to God he knew that I would never show it.

4

THE silver plane eased in to Love as they stood waiting on the apron. In his mind Pete Elliott had a picture of Ben Clark lounging in the fraternity parlor, and then someone else got off the plane. This Ben Ray Clark wore a Homburg and a pencil-thin topcoat with black velvet lapels. Behind his dark-rimmed glasses you could not see his eyes.

"Where's Cissy?" he said. He handed one of his two light bags to Elliott to carry. He told Fanch, cutting him off when the old man started to say something, to go and bring the car around by the baggage reclaim.

Clark and Elliott rode the moving walk by the yellow walls to the lobby in silence. In the lobby Pete Elliott said that he would just go on and take his own car home; he had not come with Fanch.

That was the last that Elliott saw of his friend, except at a distance. Ben Ray Clark ran the kickoff luncheon for the Henry W. Fanch Hospital, and the campaign. It was highly successful. A year or more passed. The door closed, and people stopped talking about the thing that had happened, or thinking about it much. In the early summer of that year the *Morning News* ran a story announcing that Henry W. Fanch had become honorary chairman of Texas Drilling Corporation and that Ben Ray Clark, at the age of thirty-seven, had been named chairman of the board. Rufus J. Wood, a man in his fifties who had been passed over three years before in favor of the vigorous young leadership that Clark would bring to the company, was named president and chairman of the executive committee. The story said that Mr. and Mrs. Ben Ray Clark were leaving on an extended tour of Latin America and the Near East in order to investigate new sources of oil and markets for oil equipment for TexDrill.

Peter Elliott read the story to his wife over coffee with his second cigarette of the morning.

"That's a cushy life your old buddy has worked out for himself," she said.

"Cushy?" Elliott said. He reached and speared another cigarette from the pack sitting on the breakfast table.

"I thought you were trying to give that up," said his wife.

He folded the newspaper, lit the cigarette, and looked at her.

Endzone

THE sky was Greek blue. An hour before the contest the endzone was filled. Then it was filled so tightly, much over capacity, that there was no room to move up and down the steps. Everyone was crushed into the other, like a wriggling coiled caterpillar wreathing in and out in fuzzy jerky ripples with one heart. No one could move. It was packed tight. The walls of the Cotton Bowl were shining white in the sun, looming around the pockets and smears of people like a great sparkling lavatory bowl. It was late August, brilliant blue sky-domed day of intense heat, full of the packed stirring smell of black and brown and rank white sweat, day of the hungry dog. Hot. It was an afternoon game, with the hated Packers. It was the Salesmanship exhibition game. The field below was a gorgeous striped green. The people jammed into the endzone sat and quietly laughed and talked and drank Coke and orange and Dr Pepper until they could no longer bring it down the aisles in iced paper cups, making the great snake in the bowl writhe, the colors of the beach change, the water shift its mood. Or ate meat sandwiches for lunch from sacks. Black and Latin, a few whites, they watched the sidestands fill up with the high rollers, gaining a further sense of self, *endzoners,* looking up toward harsh bright sky to see the time tick off on the great blue and silver-starred Republic clock, waiting for

27

⌐⌐

the moment when the Cowboys would come out onto the lush striped field to kill Green Bay.

I was there with the chairman of Philosophy and another friend. We ate hard white bread and dark spiced oily meat, and were drinking Cokes from iced paper cups, chewing on the ice. It was terribly hot. I wore a folded cardboard eye-shield that said, in green, HORNED FROGS, on its visor. The chairman of Philosophy wore one marked HOGS. It was red. The man on the left and just out of the lap of the chairman of Philosophy offered him a look through his binoculars. He had a mustache like Fu Manchu and was a simmering red-brown in color. Looking through the glasses my friend the philosopher noted and remarked that the grass on the field was in good shape. Several all around us affirmed that this was so. Up the aisle a thin young policeman in blue with a large belt and pistol and a visor on his cap that cocked down humorously to his nose tried to clear the steps. Everyone laughed at him good-humoredly; flesh separated in a narrow line, came back together. The fellow with the Fu found the young cop in his binoculars, then took them off him, shouted to him that he should desecrate his mother, in Tex-Mex. It was hot. A piece of ice from my paper cup dropped upon the raised shirttail of a very large black man just in front of me. It began to slide down his shirt and onto his sweating skin and I watched it slide slowly down into the dark crevice below his belt. But he did not seem to notice or perhaps he was grateful. I was glad of that.

Then Green Bay came out. There was a roar.

There were the hideous mothers, the sons of dogs and pigs and goats, the living hunks of massive bone muscle and shit that had beaten Dallas in the championship game. They were Nemesis. Had Dallas ever beaten them? Would

Dallas emerge fully erect one day and smash them, screw them down into the ground, gut them on the green lush turf? Would it be today? We rose, all fully up, endzone presenting the point of hate and noise at them.

On both sides of the stands the honkies also rose and howled whitely at them.

They split in phalanxes, came down the field to us in units, in their fancy gold and green, dispersed, pranced to throw and catch the golden balls in air. They came right down to the endzone rail, a few of them, catching the ball on fingertips, gracefully turning on the run back to grin green and gold at us.

One came, who had been a hero of the game; made a gesture to us. We howled, howled, howled.

Then they left the turf. Then the Cowboys came. We roared again. Our blue-and-silver boys. Linemen of massive thighs and arms, the weight of whose genitals could not be guessed. Black Pugh, white Lilly, fierce lithesome Lee Roy. Backs fleet as wind, strong and bold as horny bulls. Flankers, splits, and safeties. The Lance, cool and slim and sure. Bob Hayes danced before us, zephyr-footed, swiftest human in the world. We roared for Bobby Hayes, wingéd of foot, fastest man alive. Surely we would win today.

The band played. Some stood, or sang, watching the flag lie still and hot over the shimmering silver clock that said that it was nearly time. Someone yelled, at the hymn's end: "Beat Russia!" The chairman of Philosophy and I, we chuckled.

Kickoff came. They got the kick; and in a few plays then they scored. Later in the half they scored again. From the endzone hate and paper cups were thrown out on the field.

Meredith kept screwing up. The stands howled, raged, screamed bloody-eyed at him. The endzone did not mind so much. They were more loyal to their players, also hated the others more. They did not join in chanting: "*Mor*-ton. *Mor*-ton."

But when Hayes—Mister Speed, man—took a pass and began to turn it on, with a clear lane down the sidestripe, moving on so fast he left the ball behind him up the field in the grass, a dirty Easter egg, then they choked, strangled. The hydra found its voice, its rage: here was a proper goat, who was supposed to be so good.

They would have killed Bob Hayes, eaten his black flesh if they had had him then.

And with minutes shearing from the clock Green Bay came down to us to grin again and kick a field goal. The ball came arcing beautifully through the silver goals over the rail and fence into the endzone to us. It landed just two first downs to the right and above where my friends and I sat squashed together like three gray follicles in an epiderm.

They fought for it. It disappeared, as if eaten by a mouth. Police, three of them, came down two aisles after it. You could not keep the balls, they were property. Then the police disappeared too, just disappeared. Feet kicked out from under them, here, tumbling humorously down the aisles, blue legs there, blue arm, cap knocked off in air, to fall and merge with the mass. The endzone heaved, strained, laughed darkly. The tremors came along the flesh, to us.

We sat there. I think we watched the game, for it went on. No, we did not move, the three of us.

Police came, a legion of them, to the top of the endzone, then moving down. The scrambling continued to our right. "Kill them pigs!" I heard above. "Don't let them mothers come in here!" came the cry. On the field Dallas had the ball. The sidestands cheered. Young Morton trotted into the game.

Look at all them police, the large man in front of me said

to his white-toothed companion as they both shifted heads around to see. We should go rob a bank, man, with all them police here. They should go and desecrate their mothers, them police, said the man beside us.

Just up from us arose a strange man, an albino man who had two young albino children with him, his sons. He was albino and had red eyes and looked strange there amongst us, like a freak. You better cool it, he said. You better not do anything to the law. You better have some sense. You need the law. They laughed and hooted at him, but he said it all again and stood there, stood up among us with his sons, who also stood, so they could see him, and said not to mess with the law, to cool it. Off-color, sport, a freak.

The police above were coming down. The huge man in front of us stood up, turned, and looked into my eye. All around the people got up. The endzone flexed, began to writhe and turn its head up to the policemen coming down. The albino shrieked again, to let them come; and the chairman of Philosophy sank down upon his seat and began to wipe the moisture from his glasses and I stood turned toward the field and prayed for a miracle and then I saw it and, with others, shouted, shouted, and the head of the snake turned back to the field and I had seen it thrown and it was a terrible pass and bounced off someone's helmet, gold or silver, and up into the air, golden apple, free for the plucking, and he was there—Hayes, Jesus, baby—Hayes—and had it and as the endzone came around to it had dodged the remaining secondary and was gone and was even now in the endzone, leaping up and dancing down with clapping hands, tossing the sphere of pig away, and scored, and the Cowboys came to kiss him in the endzone at the far end of the field from us, in that good clean beautiful other endzone. Morton had thrown a crazy touchdown pass and Hayes, man, Hayes— Oh goddamn beautiful Bullet Bob!

31

And the kick was good.

And, in the endzone, no one recalled the police but everyone smiled and turned to suck the blood from the throat of the one next to him.

Grass

MY brother, a large gentle soul who has the humanist's mixture of contempt for human nature and concern for human beings, and who likewise is a teacher but does not like myself suffer under the burden of being a Christian, disagrees with me about the grass.

It puzzles both of us as it grows here, for our early experience of it lush and high and forever needing mowing in the spring and summer months in Ohio is far from what it is on this stone-baked land in this prairie suburb near our college. Here weeds of all kinds, weeds we cannot identify, and dark green rank crab and monkey grass thrive in those same summer months, but the thin blue Bermuda or succulent St. Augustine survive the chinches and the heat only by such feats of watering and care as I am hardly fit for, and he would never do. It is true, I must concede, that to do it right you must be a fanatic like my neighbor Nana. It is ridiculous, my brother says, to dig up all the weeds and greening bad grass out of the tan pad of turf in early spring, to make way for the better; nor would he ever help me at it. It is ever folly here, he says, to dig up anything that is green; you must cherish everything that can exist, rainless, in this hard dark waxy.

But we always agreed about the edging, on principle and according to our nature and stance to life: you must never edge, certainly not with a power tool.

Now that he has gone, returned up to the greener country, and I (strange and hard to admit) have begun to feel in me a certain desire to edge—to chop and clean the scraggle of unruly grass straight down the line of white sidewalk on either side—and Nana's fate has come to her, I begin to see this experience with my neighbor and the unending fight and tension with her in a faintly different light: sadder, paler, more like dusk than morning light.

Our tension with Nana—Big Nan—centered not just on grass. It had to do also with leaves and ivy. At root, I see now, it was quite philosophical. For that dear huge tall ungainly woman loved the neatness of her white-painted house, ruthlessly trimmed bushes, her stunted trees, her fountains, and the lush carpets of her grass. Our magnolia leaves would fall in course, and lie there (for whole *days* without our raking them, collecting them, as she would lumber off to tell the other neighbors in her fierce whisper); then they would blow over onto her yard. Invariably she, in her wild muumuu, beer can in hand, stooped at the driveway line to throw them back onto our ragged yard. And our weeds traveled over to her sanctuary, violating the thick pruned plot where, hose in hand, she worshiped and, I know now, had her only moments of peace. And, truly, we—my wife and I—were sorry for it and did our best. But we did not water, or only rarely. Nor did we cut it all down regularly, or prune, in Saturday and Sunday concert with all the others up and down the street. We were an eyesore, a blight, the cause of a grief we chose to take lightly, in that model of a trimmed and well-worked block.

And as if all the ragged house and yard were not enough, there was the ivy. Our plain small house was covered with ivy, a thirty-year growth it must have been. It grew wild, was wild, true. It had begun to finger over and in the windows, and to pry up the poorly painted planks where they met the old red brick at joints and juncture-places. Green and shiny-dark, it foliated thickly up the chimney and sprawled out above and around the chimney top like the wild heads of blacks or Indians, or great snakes dancing, or octopus arms, or dark spumes of spray on a blue, rockbound beach. I loved that ivy as Nana loved her cultured grass, and had the conceit that it was what kept the little shell of a house up, kept it from collapsing. My brother also had ivy all over, possessing, strangling, his house; and when he moved and then came back I drove him by it and they had raped it all off, hacked it down, sandblasted off the barnacle marks the ivy-suckers leave, cleaned it down to the bone of startling bare wood and brick.

"Jesus, Broth'," he said, "I wish you hadn't brought me by it." We went home and drank, a lot, to various needs and follies.

But as to my ivy, it was dirty, dusty, full, as Nana told us quite directly, of *mites.* Birds roosted in it, dirty filthy birds, and in the chimney. She was right. Several, black with soot, came down our chimney; our gentle dog killed three, leaping at them and catching them in air.

The tension came early. It was fall when we moved in, and a matter of the leaves, the huge magnolia leaves, spined and glossy on one side, brown on the other, which lie very brown and crackled like withered hands if not picked up, or blow beautifully across yards on down the street.

"I can't help it that the leaves fall," I said to her. She towered over me, a bush of hair, gauntly naked under the muu-muu, mean as hell and scaring it out of me, brandishing the hose. She had watered hours that day.

"Their falling is an act of nature," she said. "Leaving them sitting there is—is *sin!*"

"I like them," I told her. "I like the way they fall and lie there. I like the way they scatter in the wind. I don't mind your redbud leaves. You see, growing up, when we were boys—"

"*Everyone* knows how you keep your yard," she said.

That too was the truth. They all knew. In the beginning, thinking or hoping it was nothing more than a kind of egg-headed naiveté they'd had thrust into their midst, they tried to help. I had many offers of the use of power mowers and edgers, much advice on which would be best for my particular situation to buy. Those were the days when my neighbors, each dressed in gray or pink or tan coveralls and a cap to match, pushing equipment that easily might have won a major battle in the field, waved at us, would call to me, as I snickersnacked about, hoping in their goodness that I would in a moment actually begin to *do something:* "Hey there! You can come help me when you finish there." It was the street joke, the high humor of the block. I smiled and went back in to read or take a nap.

Bob came over, Nan's husband. She had married late, and married Bob. He was a little man of good heart who was delighted to be driven by her like a Trojan in the yard. He never entered any quarrels, and I believe they had a good relationship and moments of real joy. Often, weekend nights, from over their high fence where four outsize marble fountains functioned in her backyard, we heard them laughing, she right coquettishly, as they drank their beer deep into the night. Bob, with shy good humor and as if this were the first time, again offered me the use of his power edger. He had been edging, as he did at the hour of our dinnertime every third or fourth night. Edged, sliced, between his yard and walks, yard and drive, great troughs where squirrels and rabbits might have fallen in and perished, had there been any.

"Best kind to get," said Bob to me. "Sears. Hundred eighty-six bucks, but I got it on a special. So would cost you more. Listen, just feel free to use her any time. Show you how to crank her up."

The machine with its whirring blade terrified me. How many times and how pointedly had I told Bob I did not edge, did not choose to edge? But I liked Bob, Bob you had to like. He was some sort of clerk in a store, or the manager perhaps. I am sure it must be manager. So like a fool you stand and watch the operation, the old how-to, and even take the shaking popping thing an inch or two along your drive, frightened for your feet, clanging into concrete, shooting sparks.

"Any time," Bob says. You nod. And you keep on cutting with the old rattly handmower "borrowed" from the Buildings and Grounds department of the college—my neighbors had not before seen such a thing, I think, for certainly they took it for an insult to them—making uneven swipes at the grass and weeds, smoking pipe, thinking of a thousand other things. Two days later it rained and I came in the driveway inches over on Nana's grass and next morning, cup in hand, we saw her bending, screaming, cursing, throwing black clots of garden mud at the side of our old car.

The hell of it is, you know, you retaliate.

And we who tend to be so essentially aloof, preoccupied with one foolish thing or another, tend not to retaliate in kind, but in more dreadful because, let's confess, less human ways.

"Carroll," my wife said to me, "I can't stand it, that woman, anymore. She's mean. She turns on all her lights every time we come in at night, turns 'em all on every time our guests come or go. She stands and waters and *deliberately* gets it on our driveway where it makes mud in that hole, or on the car. It went in the window yesterday—"

"Yes. I got a good wet ass."

"—and she throws all the leaves back over. And she

37

stares at me through her damn shades. Then I went over there and do you know that she was sweet as pie? 'Sh,' she said, 'let's talk about it later. I know you people just live differently. Bob's asleep, let's not get him upset. Bob's been sick, you know.'"

"Well, he has."

"Yes, but don't you think we should have it out, talk it out with her like decent reasonable people?"

"Just let her be, baby," I said, "let her be. It's so important to her, let's just keep trying to do our best."

And so we did, short, of course, of changing one's whole lifestyle. I thought, rationally and clearheadedly, that we simply were not edgers, that we liked ivy. We said we were sorry for the woman. But you do retaliate.

You laugh, and tell the story many times of when Big Nan sneaks over and steals blossoms—gorgeous they were too—of your hated magnolia tree and runs back in her house with them and a friendly back-biting neighbor lady tells you of it. You give more parties and keep the guests later, knowing she's on guard. But mostly, when the tension mounts, you turn to mockery, the cutting doubleness of irony, being, really, safe and quite superior.

"Nana" was not her name, but her little niece and nephew who came to visit called her that and so we did too. (To her face we called her by her proper name.) We noted that she let the kids play free and even wild on her grass and felt better toward her for it. Finally (she lived beside us seven years) we even tried to have her and Bob over for a beer, a brew of reconciliation. That was several years ago but already was beginning to be too late, for Bob could no longer drink the beer by then. But mostly she became a story, and a funny one, to our friends and guests, who also felt her wrath if their wheels nipped her grass or they dared park in front of her house. (She would call the police or bounce them by the bumper with her own car over in front of our house, where they belonged.) We had a friend who was a poet, or versifier, and an amusing chap he was. Seeing her so many times lank and ravaged, holding her hose so determinedly for hours over her grass, he wrote a poem about her. It began: "Oh Nan / Poor Nan . . ."

"Goodnight, Nan. Goodbye, Nan! Thanks for the light, old Nan!" our guests yelled as they left, late, our house. "Shut up, you idiots," we shushed them, laughing.

When Bob had his heart attack and the ambulance came we were of course concerned. And when Nana, all dressed up in a real dress, went to visit him we tried to be outside when she came back in order to ask about him. But when he came home small and thin as a dry leaf and with the fear in his eyes we were not invited to the party on the street to celebrate his victory—not that we expected to be, or of course begrudged it. Then it seemed she would stand for hours longer, taller, more gaunt, watering in her yard.

One evening after a belt of something stronger than beer I said to her when picking up the paper in our yard how nice hers looked. She stood there for so long a time without looking at me that I thought she had not heard, and started in. Then I heard her say, behind me, in a strange and strangled voice: "It's too much. I hate it." I went on in and my wife said, "My God, can you believe she's still soaking that yard? It's nearly Christmas."

And that was about the time when Bob died, but a year later, I think from the third attack, and now it has come around to April again. Bob did well for a while; she nursed and mothered and worried about him horribly—with some justification, for every Saturday he would try to get out and cut or edge at least a little strip. He was so determined that the doctor finally said he could cut half the yard if the evening was cool and he bought a self-propelling mower. The day sticks in my mind when Bob came over to try to give me a real good deal on his old machine. Then when he was gone, Nana, as my friends in Geology say, cratered. She let the place go, making only poorly coordinated attempts even at the yard. She stayed mostly in the fenced backyard, where we could hear the water running down her fountains.

And ultimately she had to let it all go really, for she had no one—we never knew just what other family she had except the small niece and nephew whom she would go to get and then take back somewhere—and no resources to keep it up, even now to keep it.

So presently it is spring, well into spring for this part of the country, this sun-drenched essentially harsh flat land, and Nana has moved already into her apartment, though the place beside us has not yet sold. Our neighbor lady informs us that Nana is asking too much for it, and I do not doubt it. I drove by the apartment where she lives now and saw her sitting by herself on the porch of the duplex sipping at what must have been a sherry or a drink, seeming to be doing nothing but watching the sun go down. Soon we must go to visit her, if only briefly; as soon as we can prepare ourselves to do our best to know another person there.

"It's sad," my wife says, and it is. "But we tried with that woman. You know that's so, Carroll. We did try."

And that is also true. In our way, we tried.

Maybe it's not just Nana. Maybe it's the way things come together anyway as life goes on, and the timing of it all that changes the colors of your thought; maybe that I've been feeling this urge, or need, to edge, to cut things in cleaner patterns, more classic lines, and would have been feeling it even without Nana in the picture. Maybe so. I haven't yet studied it enough to know.

However that may be, I have been standing here resisting

with all my might another urge, that ultimate patronizing self-saving impulse that comes to us in the guise of love or charity: I have been stopping myself from going over to cut and trim, with the tools I have, Nana's now-ragged, wild and weed-filled yard.

I would, you see, so love to do it. But I'll be damned if I will, as I tell myself, for poor Nan's sake.

The Wind

ACTUALLY she was more promiscuous before marriage than after. Even that was the usual high school fumbling, front-seat "making out," or heavy back-seat "petting" parked outside the town of Levelland by her daddy's endless rows of vegetables and cotton. Daddy was never really rich, he was up and down, but he made it fine. He'd make it as long as the deep artesian water held out, he always said, which would be after he was gone and the Devil take the hindmost, Daddy said. She remembered most the wind blowing over the cars parked so vulnerable out there on the huge openness.

It made you want to draw closer to the boys; but then the wind would begin to blow and pick and seep around the cracks and crevices like Bobby Hightower's constant fingers going for your pants, making you nervous and half-crazy with it, anxious and afraid. Usually she would send the boys, even Bobby, home howling under the moon, staggering to their hot beds through the antsy wind suffering from "passion pains." Actually she got known in high school as a "p.t." Actually she graduated as a "technical virgin."

She remembered those dumb old terms now, my God, at nearly forty, and they seemed so funny it made her want to cry.

She went to The University, the orange-and-white one, then, and latched on to Charles and after that her life was

43

pretty much what she wanted, what she'd planned, and what Mama and Daddy had planned for her for a long time without her knowing it. Daddy was so West Texas he almost made her go to Texas Tech in Lubbock but Mama had a fit and said that would never do, she would get stuck out there with some rancher or cowboy or cuckoo. Mama was all for SMU where the rich kids went but they compromised on The University and as it turned out she ended up in Dallas anyway. Daddy said grudgingly she had better go live where her husband lived. Also that Dallas was the only place in Texas that squeaky-voiced little dip-do, meaning Charles, could be from in Texas. He said that to Mama but Bettiann heard it. To her he said directly, "Honey, this Charles you have found must be about ten years older than God."

"Why, Daddy?"

"Because he is so damn pompous and—*old*. Listen, Bet—"

"I *love* him, Daddy."

She did. Charles was kind and gentle and sweet as a boogerbear. "Kind" later turned out to be complacent and "gentle" to be almost cruelly perversely aloof to anything that might possibly interest other human beings, but that was true when they married, and you had to be fair in your rememberings. He was older, older by about seven years than the boys she had been letting French kiss her and play a little ticktacktoe on her body. Charles was already graduated from Yale and through law school at The University and was taking, real rapido, a Ph.D. degree in economics. With that combination and the family money in Dallas she—*they*—couldn't miss on making it.

And all that part had come true as rain, or wind.

Charles had been senior economist already at the bank for several years and was heavy into land investment and development besides, the latter with a Canadian company.

She read in *D Magazine* that the Canadians loved Dallas because it was the size of Toronto and had a market the size of
Australia, or something. Charles had helped Jack McGon-
nigle develop the biggest malled shopping center—bigger
than NorthPark, almost as big as DFW—in North Texas
out of what had been nothing but woods and fields at the
present far outer north perimeter of the ever-spreading
Metroplex.

They had always lived in Highland Park, moving twice.
The realtors valued their present house at close to a million dollars. Of course real estate was horribly inflated but
Charles had bought it five years before for only $236,000.
Two years ago he bought her a new ring. He wanted her to
wear it instead of the two-carat diamond he had given her
out in Levelland with Mama and Daddy sitting there when
they got engaged. It was twenty carats, with a foil of fifteen
smaller diamonds all around it. It looked like a space station
in *Star Wars*. She could hardly hold it up at first. She knew
everyone looked at it. She knew Charles wanted them to.
What the hell, she thought. Now she had a dark blue and
silver Seville and wore also a big jade ring, three gold
bracelets, and a heavy silver-and-turquoise watchband on
her ring hand, even when playing tennis. It didn't matter,
she was right-handed. On that hand she wore only the good
hard calluses from her old true-blue racket.

Lately she had persuaded poor old pompous Charles to
take up an "interest." Now he played some golf. He went to
the tournaments, the Nelson and the Colonial. He liked her
to dress up cute and come along. You had to hand it to him,
he liked to show her off. Only last year he had taken her to
a big poolside party where brewskies and bloodies were the
order of the day and where the men could enter their wives
or women in a bikini contest. She came in fourth but Charles
was real proud. "By Godfrey," he said to one and all, telling

45

about it around their own pool, "those other babes were true foxes. In their twenties. They were all Tens."

For years Bettiann had had one of those wonderful Texas women's figures. Built for jeans and boots when she was young. Long-legged and long-waisted. She had blue eyes and dark hair so if she didn't look just like Liz Taylor she didn't resemble a cow either and came pretty close to Gale Storm, if you remember her. Her only problems were that her breasts seemed to get saggy and she'd had a little dumpling double chinny-chin-chin since she was ten. She consulted with Charles and got his permission to have her breasts redone. He was pleased with the result, though he embarrassed her by talking about it. "I never heard of a boob job to make 'em *smaller*," he told their friends. "That *is* wild," said Sarah Pate, who had practically none at all.

Bettiann had come to Charles, you might say, technically still almost a virgin. At any rate, her several freshman and sophomore experiences of sex were hardly memorable, if that is a measure of anything, lost in a haze of fast driving, surfing, beer, and booze. "Going all the way" with Charles was like setting out with little fanfare and getting nowhere in particular pretty fast. He seemed distracted and would often hum. Being under Charles was like jogging to the distant predictable rhythms of the Dow Jones Industrial Average.

The wonder of it really, she thought, was that she had not had affairs. She had considered it seriously. Even now at the back of her mind she thought she owed herself one raging affair, for her fortieth. She knew how that birthday would be. Charles would have a party. Maybe he would put a big trailer-hitch signboard in their yard: BETTIANN IS 40. DOWNHILL ALL THE WAY. No, Charles would not do that. He would probably not be so thrilled that she was forty. He had not minded that age himself since he thought forty was mellow prime time, but he was dreading fifty like it was downstream beer.

The funny thing about affairs was that they were so hard to have. Nobody had affairs anymore, in Dallas anyway. They just went ahead and got divorced. Sarah Pate was just divorced, after fifteen years. She went around real sulky, smelling musky, like she was in heat. Sarah would latch on to a man real soon, if anyone could. But no one who was married had "affairs" in Highland Park. Where would you go? The Highland Park Cafeteria? The S & S Tea Room? Run down to the Longhorn Ballroom on Cadiz and Industrial? Sneak over to the Snake Pit on Harry Hines? Life was a goldfish bowl in Dallas. Everyone would see you and know. Everyone was too everywhere in Dallas, out all the time looking for diversion, giving life their best shot; everyone wherever you went who was "on the make" was so damn much younger. Affairs happened in Harlequin Romances or in *Madame Bovary* or *Anna Karenina* or on the stupid TV series "Dallas," not in Dallas.

If Wonder Man came walking down the aisle of the Tom Thumb supermarket, why, hell, you got your divorce and married him. And so on.

Whack. Whappo. Bettiann was on the court, playing doubles with the girls, with tall lean Frances and short stout Paula and skinny Ginny. They were all girls her age, except Paula who was older and had no regard for her looks. Bettiann was content that she was in a better state of preservation than the rest of them. She was content that when the fraternity boys slowed down cruising in their BMWs or TransAms they were looking at her. After tennis Sarah was taking her to a luncheon lecture. The movement, the stretching and tensing and hitting and bending and sweat-

47

ing through all your pores and parts, of tennis and the prospect of seeing the young professor who was to lecture, seeing how he would look at her, what his attitude would be on seeing her again, excited her.

There was a group of Mexican men working or pretending to be clipping bushes and cultivating flowers in the bed who were really watching them play. That was the trouble with these courts when the club was booked. Those Mexican men were usually hanging around. "They're pretty hard up if they have to watch us," dumb Paula said. She should say anything. Bettiann knew their hot brown eyes were searching to see the silk of their tennis panties tightly caught to the motion of their rears . . . Leap. Lob. Back to the net, smash it past poor hapless Ginny—

Then the boys' track meet practice in the afternoon. Life was so relentless. And that terrible party tonight, the most pretentious people they knew. You didn't mind if people were pretentious about their money, if they really had it, like all that ice sculpture that was the rage last year, at least that was something real. These people were just, well, really *pretentious* about a bunch of nothing. Smarty-asses, Daddy would have called them.

Bettiann had commissioned a large ice sculpture when Charles joined the Dallas Safari Club and went to Africa with three other bankers and shot all that stuff and had those silly heads stuffed and mounted. Charles had a big picture of his friends and himself posed with the stuffed kudus or whatever they were, horny things, and Charles and his friends looked stuffed too. She'd had an ice sculpture of an elephant. It had melted down from big elephant to little elephant pretty quick even in the air conditioning but Charles said he loved it. It was the symbol of the Republicans and they had seen elephants in Africa on safari and one had even run towards them but they had not shot it.

Bettiann was glad. Daddy liked elephants, though a Democrat. Daddy always said it was a symbol of freedom. Mama said so was the damn old coyote, for that matter.

Waiting for fat Paula to serve, it occurred to her that Dallas mostly was sun and blue sky, good sun and sky, though it had its times of fierce wind, like home, too. You could play a lot of tennis in Dallas. You could play it almost every day.

If she didn't concentrate, old fat Paula would ace her again. Now the sun was hot. The men were gone away. She could concentrate on the service. Sometimes that damn diamond on her finger weighed a ton.

Sarah picked her up before noon. Sarah's face was bloated from crying, or maybe from drinking, or both. It wasn't that Sarah wanted Henry back; she hated him. Sarah was lonely. On the way, in Sarah's new white Seville, Bettiann thought how much she would like to go out shopping instead of doing all these things she had to do. She wanted to buy a rug, an ageless old Bokhara or something. She needed a new silver chafing dish. She would redo the living room. And the den. Get that billiard table out of there. Charles never used it, no more than he used his study or smoked the fine cigars from Dunhill's that he kept in his mahogany and cedarwood canister. Redo the whole pool area, the cabanas. Make it bright and blue and yellow and orange and tawny and young-looking!

Six years ago she had taken a course from the young professor who was speaking. His name was Samuel. He was slim and reddish-haired and beautiful, really a golden boy. The course was the Romantic Poets. Shelley and Wadsworth and Keats and Sheets and Skeets and all of them. They'd done a little coke in a silver spoon in his office after class one evening and she'd said she'd meet him the next day. That was the closest she had ever come, affair-wise. (Or foolish!) She had to pick him up in her yellow Jag that no-body, of course, would recognize. Then he wanted her to go with him to an X-rated movie to "warm her up." It was hor-rible. It was a man named John Holmes with a thing as thick as a Gila monster and about three lumpy feet long. He was a gigolo, a professional screwer. He degraded women. Tense as a tiger in the stinky seat beside Samuel she stayed, with all the nasty old salesmen in there, through two epi-sodes of it. Samuel thought it was fun, funny. The episodes were almost exactly the same, just poor different girls get-ting it stuck to them like animals by John Holmes, who made horrible faces at them while he was doing it. It was wham bam, thank you, ma'am, goodbye. So when Samuel reached his arm over towards her Bettiann sprang up from the seat and knocked her blind way out to the aisle and ran out into the bright blinding sunlight of the glorious Dallas day, even though she felt horribly guilty and ashamed, and sure that Charles would be standing at the entrance of the movie theater to greet her.

Now Samuel was lecturing to them in the plush dining room of the Women's Club. He glittered among the silver and the crystal. He was definitely older by now and, she re-alized with an odd feeling of foolishness and amusement, pretty definitely gay. Oh boy. How many women had he laughed at? It did not solace her to think that maybe he went both ways. Still, she got horny listening to him and watch-ing him again, after the tennis and the hot water and the toweling. In her mind's eye she began to ride him, woman on top, damn it, like riding the mechanical bull at Billy Bob's, whoring in her heart . . . As he spoke of the origins of humanism and the painters of the Renaissance in Italy she swore he winked at her, sitting at her table in a litter of awry napkins, used plates, and dishes of melted ice cream.

The hostess thanked Samuel, said he himself was surely a

"Renaissance man." If you only knew, Bettiann thought.

Driving home, Sarah said, "I took his course in Contemporary Poets last year in the Adult Series. He's a stud, all right, isn't he? Did you see him wink at me?"

"Jesus," said Bettiann, who was brought up in the Disciples of Christ church. Daddy always said she looked most like his true precious angel in her choir robes. "I should have gone to Texas Tech."

"What the hell does that mean?" said Sarah, sulky as a goat.

And the party was terrible, too. There was an old man there who had singlehandedly created the golden image of Dallas and another who had restored the image of Dallas after the assassination and a terrible old lady who was a snob because she had written a book about the early days of Dallas. The party was full of snobs, people from most of the really old families in Dallas, whoever they were, like Charles's. She had never met so many people who claimed to have been born in Dallas in one room before, or at all.

"They should have an ice sculpture of the Dallas skyline, and we could watch it melt," she said to Charles but he didn't get it. To top it off, Charles's old aunt Minnie Lou or Minnie Haha or whatever it was got on him about how he treated his mother before she passed on—he didn't treat her much at all, just put her in a rest home—and got him thoroughly upset so he got into the Scotch after dinner and she had to drive home. Smoked a cigar too, so he stank of it.

At the party Bettiann saw a dozen old ladies in their seventies or eighties sitting in a circle. They all had withered necks and faces and arms and breasts, with all the gold and diamonds and precious stones and old family watches hanging on them like ornaments on a dead tree, jabbering away, trying to be real cute and animated, like dresses on splintered sticks, faces like dolls' with cheeks and lips and eyes painted on. Acting like they didn't know or understand that they were old.

It made her want to scream.

In the night Charles woke up and cried out. He had been dreaming. He never dreamed. She got some water and went to his room. His eyes looked nearly blind without his glasses. His nightshirt was all tangled in his legs, like a woman's gown. She patted his head and rubbed his neck a little. "Gee," he said. "I was sitting on this beach or something, on stairs I think, the top of some stairs, like Tehuacan maybe. I'd climbed a mountain—with all these guys. We were having the best time. It was a *good* dream. Then I woke up, woke up in the dream, and the water, the waves, were coming up over me from both sides—"

"Don't tell it before breakfast," she said.

He fumbled for his glasses, then took the glass of water from her without them. "Thanks, babe," he said. "You're looking good."

Two days later she decided to get the face lift.

The why of that was twofold, she might have said, trying to sound like Daddy and like Charles in the same phrase because she was uncertain within herself. Two things happened that day, anyway.

First, she and Charles went to the boys' track meet in the morning. It was Saturday. Everyone was there. It was at the new track and field named for the old mayor of Highland Park, whoever that was before the one now, whose name she didn't know. It was a grade school track and field meet, all the four grade schools competing, all the darling boys in their cute little uniforms, blue-and-gold or white-and-gold or green-and-gold or that icky drab maroon-and-gold. Fat little Franklin their younger was not competing, except in the softball throw, but Charles IV was going to run the 200-

meter and the 600-meter. He was not so really *fast* but they thought maybe he had stamina and could at least finish. He was an eleven-year-old beginning trumpeter and he had a wonderful big fine chest like his father had. Still had, it was just that now Charles had a wonderful big fine stomach too, ha ha. She put on Calvin Kleins and a cute western shirt and boots and Charles told her to wear something trickier, everyone would be wearing that outfit. Wear something Ten, babe, something that will make them know that the Cowperwoods are there rooting for dear old Armstrong School.

She made up very carefully and lavishly and wore a toga top of heavy silk material with a heavy gold necklace and a wide tie-casual gold belt and pirates' shorty pantaloons with white stockings and high-heeled gold strap shoes, with school-spirit ribbons in her hair.

She wore all her rings including the ever present Battleship Galactica and her silver-and-turquoise watch and tried to act blasé. Silly old Charles had been over to the Colonial the week before where the young girls all strutted their stuff and that day some of the idiot golfers had autographed their boobies and a tree had fallen on a man from Kansas City who unfortunately had taken off from his sales trip and was standing pretty near Charles. It was only perverse, a real private kind of gigglethought, to think how close that limb had come to hitting Charles.

This one tall good-looking honcho guy kept looking at her from different points as they would move around the field of play. Once he smiled. Some skinny fourth-grade kid threw the softball 117 feet. It was a huge field under the Dallas sun and the sky was blue as forever and the sun was gold and the field was green and she wished like fury she had a vodka martini, cool and clean and sure to the mark. There must have been a thousand parents and boys milling on the field, jumping, running, vaulting, throwing things, gawking. And here he came by again. Staring at her. Looking at her ring? Stopping— Dear Lord!

His eyes were the deepest, kindest brown she'd ever seen. He was in jeans and boots and pearl-buttoned shirt. She thought she must have known him somewhere, growing up.

"Is that a costume?" he said.

He was Wonder Man, he was Mr. Wonderful met casually on the field and that was what he said. Obviously he did not have kids here, performing, competing, wheezing and strangling around the track trying to finish the 600; he was the Spirit of her Youth, the Spirit of West Texas standing so tall and lean and cool, and he had come to see her, to rescue her. And he'd laughed at her and said, "Is that a costume?"

Which, hell yes, it was, as Sarah would say, and did, on the phone later.

Charles smiled vaguely at her as she stalked across the field, then set his face sternly and set out towards poor gasping, heaving Charles IV.

So that afternoon Bettiann changed her costume. Charles went off to a weekend meeting of his international investments group at the Anatole. They were like a Masonic lodge, a secret group, she thought they must have secret rituals, a kind of Economic Klan doing occult things to con the world markets in land, silver, gold, wheat, barleycorn, and whatnot. Charles looked his best in a three-piece suit with a slimming effect from Brooks Brothers with his Phi Beta Kappa and Golden Developer keys on the gold chain on his bulging vest and the red Canadian Maple Leaf emblem stuck in his buttonhole like he was Maurice Chevalier and it was the Legion of Honor.

She went to do the weekend grocery shopping. She avoided the Safeway in the Village where all the young ones would be, waltzing up and down the aisles in practically no clothes, like the commercials on TV for Kotex Panty Shields. She herself puttered up and down the geriatric aisles of the local Safeway, stooping for cat food, peering to price differences between name brands and Safeway's own brands, picking up sweet corn and shucking it down enough to pop a kernel with her long ruby fingernail. She wore no rings or watch or bracelets. She passed the meat counter flat by. She was going to fix a Sunday vegetable and salad dinner. Maybe she'd find some fish. Charles had eaten enough rich roasts for his fat lifetime. It was time to shape them up. Her own tummy—

"Why, Bettiann. Is that you, dear? Are you all right? I mean—"

It was old Aunt Minnie Haha, or whatever was her so-called Christian name.

"Yes. Why do you ask? I'm just—"

She glanced at the shelf by her. It was all laxatives and antacids. She felt like she was in that commercial where the poor old woman was desperately looking for relief.

"Well, if you really want to know, I was concerned because I have never seen you so—I mean, I thought you were ill, dear. I hardly recognized you. I said to Miz Sanders, down the aisle there, at Pain Relief, could that be—?"

"I am fine, Aunt— We've had a terribly busy week."

Aunt Mini-Prune-Face clucked. "Yes," she said, "you do look like a whipped dog, all right. Say hello to our dear Charles, dear, won't you?"

Home, she saw without illusion how she had gone. In truth, had meant to go. In the Mirror. Her face without makeup seemed to sag, like a jowly old querulous female dog's. Her chin, Jesus, *chins.* Lines, God, almost pouches, under the eyes. Her eyelids like a lizard's. Her nose was all right. It was a noble nose, like Daddy's. It wasn't that. She was not going to ask Charles's permission either. She would just go in the hospital and have it done. She would tell him it was something minor, like removing that old scar on her shoulder, he would approve of that, or having her sinuses drained. He would be pleased, she knew, when she did it. Look at her. A thoroughly over-the-hill, downhill-all-the-way, whipped Spaniel, on the way to Pekinese.

When she came to in the hospital she'd had a richly erotic dream of Samuel and Bobby Hightower and even Charles all rolled into one and her face and neck felt pulled to and tight, like the Chinese had operated on her and tied up her face instead of her feet. She felt panic. Would she be able to smile or talk, open and close her eyes normally, nod her head? A few days later, bandages off, relaxed, transferred to the Spring House, she made it to the mirror.

It was all right. What was it? The eyes—Was one tucked up more than the other? She had seen women who came out looking really Oriental, their eyes pulled up too tight or one pulled tighter than the other. No, they seemed to be in sync. What was it?

Finally she realized. It made her look so *young*. I mean, really, actually so, kind of like Juliet in the movie of the young, star-crossed lovers. God she hadn't wanted to look that young! *Damn* that doctor! Jesus Christ, she looked *fourteen*!

She would not cry, though. This is what she looked like now. Actually she was Bettiann. Actually she looked just about the same, except better, just smoother, younger, kind of—startled-looking—with no terrible old pouches or wrinkles. Actually—

Sarah was the first to come. She came blazing into the pretty room, all made up like a resort in the islands, telling about this funny, "thirty-nine and holding" weekend millionaire she'd met at Belle Starr's. The action for the slightly older crowd was at the C&W disco places now. Talking away like the operation was nothing. Sarah was wonderful, though she was smoking up a storm.

"How do I look?" Bettiann said.

"*Great.* Terrific. No bull, doll. It's super, a 110 per cent winner. A success."

"Come on. I've looked. Doesn't it make me look— different?"

"No. I mean, sure. Of course it does, Bet. That's why you did it, remember? It just makes you look a little—different."

Then Sarah said, too fast, not as thoughtfully as she should have, damn her, if she was going to play it out, "But as soon as I'd see those beautiful blue eyes I'd know that it was Bettiann!"

Charles called. He would come after his noon lunch appointment, he said. You needn't come, I'll be out tomorrow, or the next day. Why so long? Come and see, she said. Right after lunch, he said.

She sat in the chair in the mango-pango room with Sarah's Impatiens in a pot on the window sill of the large-paned window that looked out to a stretch of pool and green grass and gardens. Later she dozed and kind of watched "The Young and the Restless" and "Search for Tomorrow" and some of "One Life to Live." She was getting ready to watch "The Guiding Light," which was hers, the one she watched at home every day, when Charles came.

He stuck his head in the doorway to her room and looked up at the TV set on the wall and vaguely around the room, then at her. He was holding a little bunch of what looked like fresh wildflowers, Texas bluebonnets and Indian paintbrush, stuff like that, like he had stopped his car to pick them beside the expressway or something. He looked at her, poor dear gentle demanding Charles through his bottley glasses, like she was someone he had known a long

57

time ago, but now did not, and smiled apologetically and backed out of the doorway.

"Daddy!" she heard herself crying out.

But Daddy was gone. Daddy was buried in a grave that rested higher than the pure artesian water that was now almost gone and could never be replaced, in a grave in the cemetery in Levelland where the wind scours over it and wildflowers never grew.

She sat there; fumbled for the switch and shut off the soap. This was real. She sat there, willing the mask of her new face into composure, welcome. Actually he would be coming back. Unless he found Wonder Woman down the hall. Actually they would have to face each other. She wondered who the girls had got to replace her in the doubles match today.

She touched, for an instant, her breasts, her face.

The Real

NOTHING seemed very real to Holcomb anymore. Sometimes he would get up from his neat desk with its carefully arranged sheets of statistics, calculations, and analyses and look out his window. The sky would be artificially blue over Dallas; down from the tall building would be the Monopoly-block buildings below, the toy cars and buses and, he supposed somewhere down there, real people. Holcomb would try to look out over the concrete and steel-gleaming city and pick out the new freeways or other works that his buying and selling of municipal bonds had to do with. He trafficked idly in such progress in other cities too. Once in a while there would be rain or the look of high winds outside his window.

Through his thirties Holcomb was quite successful. In his mirror he looked to himself like an *Esquire* ad for a successful Southwestern businessman who might externally resemble himself. After his heart attack and recovery he had begun to become "strange" and then his wife had left him. He did not really care. They had no children and he was tired of pretending at sex. It seemed to Holcomb that he was in some thick green-glass bottle of abstraction. Now he had come south, to the Gulf, hoping that the sun, the sand, the water which he had used to love— Hoping something . . .

But it was, really, a terribly boring place. Holcomb's fathers were farmers and he wished he had gone instead back up to Missouri, to see that land again. He stayed in a place with a view right on the Gulf. The water was gentle, going from blue to green to light purple, with slight breakers, tepid, like an old man's watercolor. Occasionally a boat or ship went by, far out. The drifting white clouds in the blue sky seemed changeless, even mocking, as if perhaps they had followed him down here from outside his building window in Dallas. Holcomb went to Mexico several times to have *cerveza* and margaritas with certain of his old buddies from the University who were down there with their wives. The wives were not attracted to him, and the old buddies, talking and telling jokes in the jargon of college days like exhibits of arrested development in bottles along the bar, were boring. Then he quit seeing anyone and tried to be interested in this place where he was: to feel the hot sun burning his fat fair face and body, to feel his soles burning on the hot sand at midday, to walk up to his neck into the water and then duck his head in it and know in his eyes and mouth that it was full of salt, and bitter.

It was a rather interesting place, he supposed. It was a thin strip of sand going down the coast, bay on one side, Gulf on the other. Where he was it was not quite a mile across. Cannibal Indians had once wandered here, and shipwrecked Spanish sailors, and off there somewhere, they said, were sunken treasure galleons. Mexican nationals were mostly here staying on all sides of him, long strings of brightly robed families who came out at dusk to take their grandmothers and grandfathers to the water. He wished, as they sat out around him in the evening, that he might speak to them but he had little talent for the language and no energy for the effort.

This place was called in their romantic liquid tongue the Father Island. The bay side was Laguna Madre. In the calm waters of the bay a good or even an indifferent fisherman—

mostly the Anglos who had to have activity—could catch, any day, many kinds of fish.

Holcomb wandered up and down the beach side and the tacky garish bay side, growing more restless and more bored. Nothing happened, or would happen. He sank down in the sand and, reading some poor trash, stopped going in the water, letting it become just a picture in his mind, a background rhythm in his ears, like the dull pictures on the walls and the piped-in music of his building.

One afternoon a group of Mexican youths walking on the beach began to shout and wave wildly towards the water. Holcomb sprang up, running to the lip of waves to see. "*Tiburón, tiburón!*" they shouted, pointing out upon the Gulf. Looking, Holcomb saw the creature, then several more, that they pointed at, and he turned away in disgust at them. Those weren't sharks out there. Holcomb could tell porpoises when he saw them. Or were they dolphins? Holcomb lay back down upon *la playa*. In his heart he wished they had been sharks out there. He would have given anything if they had really been sharks.

One night he decided he would go fishing. He had done just about everything else up and down the tawdry bayside strip. He went to the worst-looking place that he could find. It was called Indian Bay. It had a lighted dock out over the smooth black stinking water and the old woman who ran it furnished you pole and bait. She was gnarled and tall and smoked and coughed and spat into the water constantly. At first he thought she was a man. She was old and filthy, in jeans and shirt, and smelled worse than the water or the heads and bits of fish decaying along the boards of the dock. You sat on a hard wooden bench and held your pole out in the water waiting for the pike, trout, and flounder she growled were surely there. Looking at her brown snarly little persimmon face as she went gimping by under his

61

dock light Holcomb thought she must be the Indian of the Bay, or something like.

He could not cast and kept snagging his line around or under the dock and losing his bait. Then he would have to walk down the splintered wood way and get another minnow. No one was catching anything, except crabs, and most of the people left, not happy. As he tromped heavily down to the bait stand again he heard her say to someone of him: "He's a pier-pacer and a bait-dipper. Wastin' my bait. It takes a fisherman to catch a fish. Diddlers and dawdlers don't catch fish."

It did not bother him. He rather enjoyed the old fool's insulting him for his ineffectiveness at the dock. He felt that if he could talk to her she might tell him many stories. And he was enjoying the farce of fishing too; somehow it was good to have his line out somewhere in the black water, to have the reel in his hands.

A young boy got tired of catching nothing and began to walk up and down the dock. The old woman came and put her claw on his shoulder, just by Holcomb. "Don't pace the pier, sonny," she said.

He shrugged away, then stood still beside her, staring out at the dark water under the black night. It was still and very hot. She lit a weed and coughed, strangling deep in her throat.

"Do you ever have any sharks here?" the kid said.

"Yeah," she said. "Occasionally."

"I think I just saw one," he said. "Right there."

They, and Holcomb, looked. In a moment he saw a movement out in the water, coming in. Something seemed to pass not too far from them, about a dozen feet off the pier. It seemed white, or perhaps it was the lights.

"Jesus Christ," he heard the old woman say, low in her throat. "Christ! Be quiet. Look."

She pointed out, like radar, now to the line of sandbar about thirty feet out in the bay, just where the bay widened and grew deeper. "Christ!" she said again, and went into her coughing, and then Holcomb saw it too—they could all see it then—for the great white instantaneous blur of tail and fin and snout rolled in upon the foot or two of clear water on the sandbar, seemed to hit and bump and grin and hang there for a long moment, all deep white and exposed to their eyes; and then the shark righted, and sped off the bar. There was a moment's fin and he was gone.

It was the most beautiful, powerful thing that Holcomb had ever seen.

In a moment, sitting in silence up over the dark water, they all turned to the Indian woman.

"That was a shark, all right," she said. "Did you see that big mother? We ain't had shark in this bay since '64. He must of come a long way, in under the bridge at the causeway. Now he smells the bait and he won't leave. Jesus. You seen that shark, didn't you?"

She turned to Holcomb. He nodded. He had seen it.

"You seen that big white mother. Must be seven foot. You seen its whiteness. That ain't just the reflection of these lights. You seen them white fins. That is a lemon shark. I never seen one before. But I am sure. A lemon shark."

She looked down at the boy. "That is the kind that would like to eat you," she said.

Then she said that she had better catch that shark, that she was closing up her dock.

Holcomb hung around after the others had left. "You get the hell out of here," she said to him and limped into her little shack office-store. Holcomb, amazed at himself, thrust through the screen and followed her inside.

"Well?" she said, very old and gnarled and vicious-looking, going towards an old desk where he was sure she had a gun.

"Listen," Holcomb said, lying. "I'm a magazine writer and photographer from Dallas. We do a state-wide magazine to attract tourists to Texas. I have my camera in my car. I'd like to stay and watch you get this shark, do a feature story on it."

"In a magazine? What for? To tell people we got sharks in In'ian Bay? Hah!"

"To show the—excitement—of it. Show how you bring it in when you do. That it's—rare, but— You don't really think a big lead story in a state-wide magazine would hurt you, do you?"

She squinted at him, lit a cigarette, and coughed. Then she went to the ice chest and took out two cans of beer and put them on the table and sat down. He sat down too and palmed the beer.

"What's the name of it?"

"Oh," he said, and made up something. He really did have a fair camera which he could work in his car, with flash equipment, and went and got it. He felt bad to be lying to the woman but could not seem to help it. He asked her for a notebook and she produced a schoolboy's pad and he began to fake asking her questions about herself and Indian Bay.

Her name was Victoria Elena Keno and she was from Oklahoma, or was it Arizona? She was full-blood Apache or half-breed Kiowa. (After a while he hardly knew the difference between what he made up in his remarks and questions and what she made up in her replies. She was, it seemed, anything he wanted her to be, anything that might sound best in his magazine.) She had been here many years.

In '64 there had been many sharks in here. That was the only year of so many. Pro sharkers had come in to catch them. Some had been six, seven feet. But this one was as big, or bigger. There had never been any white shark before. Now she would try to catch this one, this lemon, herself.

"And I'll help," Holcomb said.

"You just stand back away. You can watch but you keep back."

She showed him a picture of the eight-hundred-pound turtle caught at Indian Bay in '60, with a young girl riding on its back. "That was my girl," she said. "She went away."

Holcomb took her picture. A tall old man in khakis came in and got himself a beer. "Go easy on that, Mel," she said. "It ain't water, you know." She told Mel that Holcomb was all right, he was going to write them up. Mel was the deputy. Holcomb sat out then with his beer on the dock watching the still unrippled surface of water under the yellow lights and listened to Mel tell of his wife who was a Campbellite who thought she was going to heaven and everyone else was going to hell. Old Keno was okay, though. She'd let a man snitch a beer. You didn't want to get on the wrong side of that old woman, though, in bed or otherwise.

Holcomb felt Mel's hand lightly for a moment on his knee, and quivered.

Then a car crashed down the gravel to the dock ramp and a white-haired young man and a young girl in jeans got out. He had a large rod and reel and went right onto the dock.

"Use that big piece of flounder there, James," Victoria Elena called. "Take it to him," she said to Holcomb, who went and got the stinking bloody thing and took it to the fellow. The woman winked at him, standing with him and the girl and Mel, when he came back. "Got these newlyweds out the sack," she said. "Hah?" to the girl.

"That's all right," the girl said, flipping herself on out to where James was plunking and thrashing the water with the bait. "We done it five–six times already."

The old woman said that they could have another beer if the law didn't mind; it wasn't every night that you spooked up a lemon shark out there.

Later Vito came, a sharker who had heard of it, and then Mac and Manuel.

"Now we'll do it," she said. "Vito, he's got a sixty-pound test leader line, that's what you'll need to have. James couldn't catch a turtle with that thing of his. Manuel caught a shark off Mexico last month, he's got five heavy riggings or so. We'll get that beauty. See old Vito, he knows how to slap that water with the bait, he's got that old longjohn. *Put it out on the sandbar, Vito.* Tomorrow we'll get some real good bloody bait. *Keep her plunkin', Tiger!* That shark can smell a real good bloody bait from the causeway, mister, a distance of five miles. Say, you ain't asleep, are you? When you snooze you lose. You got that flashbulb on your camera there? You better be ready for when the mother comes rolling on back in."

"Don't worry," Holcomb said. "I'm not asleep."

But they saw no more of the shark that night.

In the morning Holcomb hurried back to Indian Bay. He knocked on the shack door, and finally Mel came to the door. "Ain't no shark going to come in here in daylight," he said disgustedly and shut it in Holcomb's face.

Holcomb paced the beach, staring at the calm blue Gulf. He walked in shorts under the deep kiss of the bright sun, terribly impatient for the time to come to watch them catch the shark. From time to time he could not believe that they—that he himself—had actually seen a great white shark, gliding to and then suspended, long and beautiful, upon the bar. He made himself hold off till nine o'clock and then went back.

They were all there, and some others, drinking beer.

"Where you been?" Victoria Elena said. "You missed a little action, mister."

"What?" For God's sake, what?

"Well, he's out there. He ain't gone away. We know that. James, he hooked him, while ago. The id'ot. I told him he couldn't catch nothing with not but a fourteen-pound test line on that thing of his. But he hooked him. It was Mister Shark all right. Like to tore James out into the water taking it and breaking it. Jesus God. Shark been hooked before, Manuel says. That's a touchy, sore-mouthed shark. Vito's going to fish for him all night."

In several hours he was alone with the old woman watching Vito plunking for the shark. Then Vito went out in a boat, plunking. "We need that bloody bait," she said. "With a bloody bait we could diddle her up into the lights again. You remember how she looked, them bright white fins? Best shark bait would be a coyote soaked in blood. How we caught mountain lion, to home. Wished I'd had my bow and arrow when that fool James hooked her. If I had fourteen days I could soak them arrowheads in this poison I know how to make— That would paralyze that sneaking fish-spookin' mother!"

The next day Holcomb saw Mel in a cafe in town. "Nah, James never had that shark," he said. "Says he just probably snagged something. That old Keno lies like hell. She's a sly old wolf. A shark ain't a bad thing to have goin'. You just watch her open up her dock tonight."

It was true that she let people, for the old fee, on her pier that night, till midnight. The word was out and a lot of people came. But it did not matter to Holcomb: he believed in the shark. He *had seen* that shark, the whiteness of it, felt in his blood the power and the beauty of it . . .

"Don't you worry," she said. "We'll get that thing tonight. We got the bloody bait tonight. Vito's going to take it out, put it on that bar, do what we should have done before. Listen—"

She told him why didn't he help Vito take it out there?

Holcomb, half loopy from six or seven beers, staggered to his feet. He received the batch of bloody bait from her. Vito brought the skiff around, using one long oar to handle it. Fat, fearful, old, Holcomb lumbered into the boat with it. The boat lurched, Vito kept the oar down and held on to the pier. They did not overturn. Holcomb sat. "You are not such a very good sailor," Vito said, laughing lightly.

They rowed out into the darkness of the bay away from the lighted dock. Holcomb shook; he sat upon the narrow boat seat clutching the bloody bait that the shark could smell from five miles off, clutching it like a baby to his breast. Jesus, he said to himself. Jesus God.

By the cool pale image of the sandbar Holcomb half-rose to hand the dripping bait to Vito. He almost tipped the skiff again. Vito laughed—or drew in his breath sharply. "Take care," he said. "Keep the eye out for our friend."

Gently he lowered the bundle of bait upon the sandbar.

Then Holcomb saw the great white lemon—or thought he did. Was it not the same long powerful flash of white, off a bit away from them, the fin—? And then he saw himself, no, felt himself, going over, the creature coming towards him, the feel of the bitter brackish water over him, the grin of death . . .

Vito rowed them slowly back up to the dock, where, shaking, Holcomb climbed up from the boat.

"You all right?" Victoria Elena Keno said. "I thought maybe I seen him just then circling around out there. You care for a beer, mister?"

Holcomb sat with her up on the dock till dawn. The white shark, who was surely out there now, did not choose to hit the bait.

Two days later Vito gave it up. She said though that Manuel was coming back, to try for him all night. The curious crowd on the night dock dwindled. Fishing for the trout and pike and flounder in the evening was almost back to normal. The old woman paced the pier telling them all to keep an eye out for the great white shark.

After the seventh night of watching for the mother, when only James was occasionally plunking a flounder bait out towards the bar, Holcomb thought that he must leave, go home. He was a day or two over his vacation time, missing appointments, losing money. He thought that, really, he could go back to Dallas now. His wife had even written him, asking how he was. He thought that perhaps he would take the heavy metal paperweight that sat upon his desk and smash the window of his building, stand and breathe the air as he watched the clouds and sky out his window, viewed the progress and the people down below.

That morning, a Sunday, early, he drove a last time down the gravel road to the pier at Indian Bay. He knocked at the door of the old office-shack. She came to the door, peered at him, and then came out into the sun. And suddenly a film fell from his eyes and he saw the shack and her quite clearly.

It was gray, and cracked, and wind- and water-stained. She was older even than he had imagined, her face not a persimmon or a prune or fig but the relic of a human face. She was the Indian of this bay, all right. He had brought his

69

camera to take a last picture of her as a gesture, but he let it hang down by his side. He told her that he would have to go.

"Hah," she said. "If you could of stayed, we would of caught that mother. Vito's coming back, tonight, with a new rig. Ah, my daughter would of known the spell, like she done in '64—"

He nodded at her.

"Well," Victoria Elena said, wrapping up around her the shabby kimono that had once been gaily flowered, "you give me your address, at your magazine, I'll send you a picture of it when we get him."

He wanted to blurt out that he was not, not at all, what she thought he was. And suddenly, also, he thought that she, who knew so much and was able to manufacture all the rest, knew that. So instead he said: "You know, sometimes I wonder if we really saw it, that thing, a week ago . . ."

She almost went back into her snarl, then looked at him quite straight, black old eyes a bead to his, composed.

"Sure we seen it," she said. "It was a white lemon shark, biggest devil ever to come in here. He's out there now. We'll get him, don't you worry none about that. If you can see 'em you can catch 'em. I want to assure you, mister, that goddamn shark was real."

Holcomb stepped forward to her and embraced her. As he kissed her the deep fish-and-filth stench of her almost made him retch, and as in his arms she coughed he could feel a deep spasm pass through the frail bag of flesh and bones he held.

The Silvering of Trees

THAT New Year's? Yes, I remember. Many do. That was when I lost faith in Dallas Power & Light. Before that, I guess I was one of the most optimistic, wimpiest citizens around. I felt that, even with Little Grinny in there, our society, our setup, was still basically right, that somehow we could handle our problems, energy and all the rest, and not break down, that America would still turn out to be a winner in the long run. I thought, till then, that this new movement was mostly crazy, mostly a haven for extremist nuts and malcontents. I still believed in "Ronnie" Reagan and "Bill" Clements and felt that if we got some strong guy like that in there we could straighten out the dollar and inflation and the whole ball game. I even thought, before the Ice Age came and the lights went out on that New Year's Eve, that Dallas would win the NFL and Houston would win the AFL and we'd have two Texas teams in the Super Bowl and that would be a big thing for Texas. That was the level of my thinking at that point in time.

But, believe it or not, this is about the trees. What happened to the trees when the ice storm came. How they cracked and split and their branches shattered under the heavy load of ice. How they *looked* then, broken and sheathed in the crystal ice. It was a beautiful, cruel thing. It shook and frightened me.

I flew home from New York City the night before that

71

New Year's Eve. It had been a good meeting. Dallas led everyone else in profits. Dallas was big right then up there, we had just stolen their precious airline. I spent the whole time in the hotel. It took them a couple hours just to get a pot of weak coffee up to the room. God, I was happy to get home from that crazy place that our tax dollars were keeping from going down the drain. New York was a place no bigger than DFW with ten million idiots packed in it, going nowhere. It began to rain and freeze as I was driving home from DFW.

I woke up, vaguely cold, at 3:00 A.M. As I looked up to see my wife Claudine standing in her robe at the window there was a flash and flare of brilliant light beyond her. She stepped back and turned her face to me and did not look like the woman I married but like an old woman who had been electrocuted. Then everything went black and it grew colder. We stood at the window of our upstairs bedroom and watched another transformer go out in a flash of fire and listened to the snap crackle pop of branches breaking and then the huge crack and crash as the ancient hackberry between us gave down the middle and knifed into our neighbor's roof. All night long, trees broke all around us and all over Dallas and at dawn they looked deformed as they glittered, silvered and crackling in the wind, in the pale cold sunlight.

I need to explain about the trees. How those few of us who are Dallas natives feel about the trees.

This is the prairie, you must understand. This is the meridian where the tree line ends. This was a hard and dangerous place to found a town, to build a city, prey to capricious temperature and howling wind and Indians. The Wichita turned back east from here, the Cheyenne and Comanche turned back west. The Trinity is no river really, but only a trickle of hope, or folly. This was a hard place to bring civilization, to build a city, to grow and nurture trees. Out north of us, on the former cotton fields, where young suburban cities run into each other and a half-million people crowd together now, every cracked and broken tree was worth its weight in gold at the current market rate.

I said this was about the trees. I am remembering it now and it seems to be about my anger, which has grown. But then I truly think it was the trees, so beautiful and broken.

So that was how and when the outage came. The outrage began with the New Year.

That morning, New Year's Eve day, we made coffee for our neighbors to the left of us. We all had gas central heat but the thermostats worked electrically. The street, the block, all around us were out of electric power. Claudine in her wisdom had not gone "total electric," she had a gas stove. My neighbor and I wandered out like boys looking at the damage. The hackberry had cleaved his roof. My big back oak was split, the telephone line dangling in it. His front pecan tree lay, cracked in half, over the top of my car which I had foolishly left out of the garage in my happiness to be home. Claudine's crepe myrtle stood like shattered lances. All the trees hung low with ice, on some it looked like there was more ice than tree. The worst we'd ever seen, we told each other. The top of my other neighbor's magnolia tree, with its frozen glossy leaves, had cracked and cratered. It looked like some Old South woman all dressed up in a hoop skirt with a broken neck. All our farther neighbor's great pecans were broken. He had trimmed them carefully so only the large limbs remained and now they lay crazily on the ground or jaggedly jammed into his roof. His individual power line lay sparking and hissing in his backyard. We hurried home to our own devastation, like boys who'd seen a snake. My neighbor buddy said he'd loan me a saw so we could cut his pecan tree off my car.

73

Everything stayed frozen silver.

Then Claudine began to grow angry with me. I looked out at it in a daze, full of faith in DP & L. We could not see them but surely they were working on it. I had no saw. My logs were huge and green and wet. I had no proper kindling, could hardly keep a fire going. I was not handy, or resourceful, or prepared, like my neighbors were. Ed McMahon to the left bought everything Mr. L. L. Bean offered in his catalogue. Daddy Ewing, to the right, was a hunter and a camper. He had a Coleman stove and a kerosene lantern, the other had a battery-operated radio. I did not even have a flashlight. I walked to Skillern's and they were out of flashlights and out of transistor radios but I got some candles.

It was Sunday. I told Claudine I would take her to the Hilton or Holiday Inn for New Year's Eve. It was going to be fifteen degrees. She said no, she'd stay home if I could make a proper fire, she didn't want to be with all those crazy drunken Irish that had invaded Dallas. I walked over and bought a small bundle of dry wood at Tom Thumb for $1.99. A huge limb of a tree cracked to the ground behind me as I walked down the street, shattering and stinging me with silver bits. That evening we watched half a bois d'arc crash out into our street. There was a line of these magnificent great trees—bois d'arc, or Osage orange—along our street from the days before wire when they were used for fence. They were the toughest wood I knew. We could not believe one could give and crash like that.

I borrowed Ed's car and drove over to see about my mother. On the way I passed the campus. My father helped found that college and my own class planted the grove of live oak trees by the auditorium. They were all over broken. It looked like some giant had come along and snapped them down the middle with his thumb and fingers. I had loved that grove of lovely live oak trees, it meant something to me.

My mother—I was just fifty-five then, she was eighty-two—sat huddled by her gas oven in her cold apartment, aching and warming towels and pillows for her neck and joints in the oven.

"I wouldn't do that, Mother," I said. "You might burn yourself up."

"Get them to turn my electricity on," she said.

We lit candles and had a little fire and drank champagne—no trouble chilling it—on New Year's Eve. Outside, the silvery trees were beautiful in the coldness and blackness of the night.

New Year's Day our neighbor's line still lay live in his yard. No one could get through to DP & L or the police or fire departments.

"No one seems to be in charge," Ed said. "The radio stations are too busy broadcasting ball games to tell us what's going on." He was getting angry because he couldn't see the Bowl games. Ed drove around and reported he had actually seen a crew working over on Greenway. Every few minutes, he said, they would climb down from the poles and watch the game on their portable TV.

On Tuesday Claudine cried because her indoor plants had died. It was that morning that the little boy miles from us was electrocuted in his alley by the live wire that had lain there exposed for days. I think I would have joined the gang of neighbors who beat the power people who came to fix it senseless with their ax handles. That day I skipped work, our profits being what they were, and went to Target and bought an ax and saw and lantern and heavy-duty flashlight and a kerosene stove. I also bought a longbarrel eight-shot .22 revolver, and ammunition.

The power, that time, was restored, of course. When I

called for time and temperature after they fixed the phone line the voice said, "Dallas—Always Building for the Future." The thaw followed. Then the trees did not look beautiful and silvery, they looked wounded, ugly. We lost so many and made hideous so many more. The piles of tree debris lined the streets for weeks. My neighbors and most people in Dallas tried to trim them or have them trimmed and pruned so even the broken ones might still have grace, some beauty, a civilized, aesthetic sense.

I lopped mine as I could, crudely, and left them that way, scarred and raw, as signs of my wrath and my intention.

Notes to the Story

"The Silvering of Trees"—critics disagree about the effectiveness of this title for the story. Yet the paradox of themes, and of the beauty and brokenness of the trees, is clearly stated in the story.

"That New Year's?"—New Year's Eve 1978 and New Year's Day 1979. During the night of Dec. 30, 1978, the worst ice storm in 30 years hit Dallas. There was millions of dollars in tree damage and 75,000 Dallas homes suffered black-outs, some lasting more than a week.

"Little Grinny"—by context a probable reference to President Jimmy Carter.

"a winner"—common Texas expression of the time, related to the idolatry of sports.

"this new movement"—the people's Anti-Tax Movement, which became dominant in American politics in the next decade.

"'Ronnie' Reagan and 'Bill' Clements"—an apparent reference to the American political phenomenon, stimulated by Richard M. "Dick" Nixon, of political figures wanting to become known by their short-form instead of formal first names. The desired effect was to suggest to the voters that the personage was somehow human and so could understand the average person's problems. "Jimmy" Carter was president at this time; the mayor of Dallas was "Bobby" Folsom. (William P. "Bill" Clements was a wealthy man who spent some $7 million in winning the Texas governorship in 1978. To some at that time he seemed to personify the vanished virtues of the frontier.)

"their precious airline"—American Airlines. In late 1978 American submitted to Texas inducements to move its headquarters from New York to Dallas–Ft. Worth. The move caused a measure of consternation in New York.

"no bigger than DFW"—Manhattan was roughly equivalent in area to the Dallas–Ft. Worth Airport.

"the meridian"—the 98th meridian, actually more in line with Ft. Worth than Dallas, defined by Walter Prescott Webb and others as the beginning of the continent's semiarid lands, which required different kinds of tools and skills to settle and sustain than the more timbered lands to the east.

"Ed McMahon . . . Daddy Ewing"—bluff emcee of "Tonight" show and character in fictional TV series "Dallas." Both names probably used ironically and not literally by narrator and author.

"crazy drunken Irish"—Notre Dame fans. Notre Dame defeated the University of Houston 35–34 in the Cotton Bowl in Dallas on Jan. 1, 1979.

"Tom Thumb"—local grocery store chain serving customers of all sizes.

"bois d'arc . . . along our street"—probably Lovers Lane, once just that, subsequently a major east-west thoroughfare. The street was known for its line of very old bois d'arc or Osage orange trees. If so, the street name, to those who might identify it, would contrast ironically with the present mood and character of the narrator.

77

"the campus"—Southern Methodist University, the only college or university campus strategically placed within residential Dallas per se. This would tend to confirm the placement of the narrator's house on Lovers Lane, a street close to the campus. SMU's founding heritage, with its religious and humane values, may be what the narrator has in mind when he says "it meant something to me."

"neighbors who beat the power people . . . senseless with their ax handles"—apocryphal, or a dramatic heightening of a real incident for fictional effect. On Jan. 2 in Dallas an eight-year-old boy was killed by a live wire that had lain for two days in an alley and been reported to the power company. The boy's neighbors were critical of the company, but no such violence occurred.

"longbarrel eight-shot .22 revolver"—target pistol (bought from Target) of remarkable accuracy. At that time anyone could buy any gun for any purpose in Texas.

Gretta, Claude, and Sally

THERE is no reason to put together the stories of Gretta, Claude, and Sally except that I knew each one of them and each in turn knew the other and that each, in a certain way, is similar. And so if you will bear with me I will tell about each of these not very interesting persons in turn.

Gretta—Gretta Grace was her whole given name and sometimes she insisted on the whole of it—lived in a duplex in a nice section of Lakewood over by White Rock Lake. At times, when she was still driving her old but large and powerful Thunderbird, she would go over to the edge of the lake, on high blue sunny days, and watch the water ripple slightly, or watch the whiteness of the small sailboats drifting on the water. But she was seventy-seven now and could not see or hear well and her driving was a terror and though she seemed to think that the good mayor, whose fine bland face she liked so much and who had known her late husband Alfred, had given her a special permission to run through red lights and stop signs, she was discouraged in her driving by her neighbors. And lately she had desisted from it, except for her food and liquor run over to the square once a week; for she knew her mind often wandered now, and she had little strength anymore except in almost manic or maniacal spurts, and then there were the spells, of dizziness or fainting. Gretta Grace had no intention of getting out and doing something public that would put her in anyone's eyes, for she knew that they were after her, knew that her only living relative, a truly horrible boy who had let the family, let them all, down by not marrying or having children, by going into a horrible queer profession, wanted to put her away, have an excuse to shut her up and make her die. He wanted her things. Well, he would never get them, terrible sick perverted boy. She would leave them to—something, someone.

Still she took the risk and went out once a week, roaring out of the garage and driveway and down the shady street very fast in the old immaculate but dented Thunderbird. You had to, you know, get out sometimes.

Several times when she did so she almost ran over one or the other of my friends the Hendersons, who lived in the apartment of the duplex over her, without even seeing them. Often, in various ways, she caused my friends concern.

"Sometimes we don't hear her move around down there for days on end," Betty Henderson said. "Twice I've called that nurse friend of hers to come and see about her. She locks herself in and won't even answer her phone. Then she keeps the TV on all the time so it's impossible to hear anything, for her to hear or anyone to hear her, anyway. Sometimes I lie up here in bed at night and just know that poor crazy old woman is dead and that we won't know about it for days or weeks probably—that we won't know until we start to smell her decomposing."

"Not that we'd notice too much different," Bob Henderson said, grasping his glass with a shrug and a look to the heavens.

But we'd all had several rounds of drinks when they said that, and they were not really cruel people but tried to keep track of the woman below, and to have concern for her.

"She's quite a character though," Bob said. "I must say I admire the old gal's pluck."

Bob was a components engineer with TI and one of the most humane and personable of that breed that I knew in this or any other city.

Gretta—Gretta Arnold, whose late husband Alfred was a banker in one of Dallas's tallest buildings and who had grown rather wealthy at it—was indeed a "character," though I doubt that she thought of herself as such or really tried to be so. Very few people really do. But the times I saw her, would stop to say a word or two to her—at which times she invariably thought that I was Bob—she certainly qualified as such. A year or so ago, perhaps suddenly thinking that she must keep the little yard of the duplex as Alfred had kept the large yard of their spacious North Dallas house, she had ordered a truckload of sand to be dumped into the yard; and we found her one evening out pushing at it with a rake, in her old torn and soiled housecoat and wearing an impossibly large and floppy sun hat with bright ribbons on it. But she was sweet, and gracious in a way, and often I am sure yearned desperately for company. At Christmas or on other holidays—once on Memorial Day—she would ask the Hendersons to come down for a drink with her, and once she even had a bridge party. It was on these occasions that my friends would see her place, her apartment, which was always just the same and quite incredible.

They would go down for the drink, and leave as soon as possible. It was the smell more than the clutter, they said, an odor impossible to describe: a smell of old lady, neglected humanness, perfume, whiskey, of sweet and sour suffocation, a smell of death-in-life.

She really had some lovely things. Antique chairs and

tables, mirrors, Oriental rugs, china bits, paintings stacked around the walls, things like that, said Betty, who was not good at precisely naming them. The woman had everything that had mattered to her scattered, stacked, and strewn about in the apartment.

She seemed to have an endless supply of liquor but not in the merchants' bottles, for that would not be ladylike and anyway she liked to keep it mobile for carrying in one or another of her large old shiny patent leather or alligator purses. Alfred had given her a purse, it seemed, for nearly every anniversary of their life together and so she had dozens of them. She kept the liquor in small plastic bottles which often had held perfume or something else first. The drinks she served the Hendersons—granted in rather beautiful old crystal water goblets, for she was not chary of putting her things to use—usually tasted like perfume.

It was true she kept the televisions on, mostly to the same station but at times randomly, not synchronized. She had four sets, two large color televisions and two smaller black-and-whites, in the living room, dining room, kitchen, and bedroom of her spacious, filthy, carpeted apartment. Once Betty Henderson, after a drink with her, presented herself the next day, plucking up her interest and her courage, and offered to help find for Gretta someone to come and clean for her occasionally. But Gretta would have none of that. She was terribly afraid of black people, of being raped or robbed; she wanted no black nigger girl coming in to steal from her. Then it was she took Betty into her bedroom, her large old bed with beautifully carved headboard piled with musty, rancid quilts, and showed her Alfred's gun. It was a .38 Police Special, loaded, with the safety catch carelessly off. She told her she might look feeble but she knew how to use it, too. It frightened Betty.

Over their drink they would talk, or listen to her tell of

her programs, her "stories"—"The Edge of Night," "The Secret Storm," "As the World Turns"—what was happening to whom. She told about the people in these programs with glee and love and hate and fascination. They were very real to her. That was the most real world she had.

Gretta Grace's bridge party was the damnedest thing Betty Henderson had ever got in on. For the life of her she could not think why she had agreed to go, she said that she must be getting soft in the head as well as heart.

And truly it was a poignant sad affair. Where Gretta had dug up the other two old ladies—although she supposed they must be former friends of Gretta's, also widows now—Betty could not imagine. They were not seen around there before or since. That time Betty spent more than an hour there, in early summer, in frightful heat—Gretta had no air conditioning and kept the windows nailed shut—until the dreadful "party" just dissolved. Gretta served sherry from the plastic bottles and had tried to make a salad of tuna fish, tomatoes, other things. It had not turned out well, that is edible, though Gretta Grace said it was according to an old recipe of her family. (Her family was an old and well-off one in Tennessee, Memphis indeed; she had always known and had lovely things, and friends, advantages.) That afternoon she dressed in old-fashioned flowing musty silk, wore pearls, did up her hair, came at them with eyes blackened hollow, spots of rouge awry on her old cheeks, her mouth a deeply painted red. It was horrible enough, and Betty was sorry but much as she did not want to hurt the woman's feelings she was the first to leave, to flee up to her fresh glorious air conditioning and mix an icy clean and burning Scotch. And the others left soon after.

When then Gretta began to have her spells of falling out, and after Bob found her once unconscious out back by the garbage cans and drove her to the hospital, and she had re-

83

covered and come back, he got up his courage and resolve and had a talk by phone with the real estate woman through whose office they rented. He began to explain his fears for, about Gretta, for her own safety, for theirs—for also she smoked loosely, constantly, he had a dread that she might burn them down—and was about to suggest that, in the light of everything, might it not be wiser for Gretta, for her own sake . . . ? And found out, as he might have known, that Mrs. Arnold, Mrs. Alfred Arnold, owned the duplex and was very careful whom she let them rent the upper to— So that was that.

And so Bob and Betty were thinking very seriously of moving themselves, even of buying a house of their own high as the interest rates were if they could get into the Park Cities, when Gretta died.

I saw her, strange to say, on the evening of the day she died. I came by to pick up Bob for softball but missed connections. He had already gone on with Ted Ormsby and Betty had gone to her bowling league. It was early evening. I saw Gretta Grace in the garage, bent over in a ratty old cardigan that had been Alfred's, digging in some of the boxes she kept stored in the open garage that faced the street. I'd driven in the drive and startled her. She came toward me, peering, even so, and I got out of the car, seeing Bob was gone, to be polite. She came up to me, her jaw working, talking, to me, to herself, smelling strongly of Vicks salve, bourbon, and perfume. She talked to me for several minutes, peering, without her glasses on, thinking I was Bob. She was in a tirade of despair and scorn over her useless horrible nephew; he was not going to get her things. He need not think that he could come around and make it up with her, either. Until she turned and wandered, shuffled, off, back into her house.

When the stroke hit her she had tried, as it turned out, to

reach help by phone. Dialed the hated thing, trying to get her nurse friend but the nurse friend's teenage daughter was on the phone and Gretta could not reach her. She tried to call her, then, even though she knew full well in her heart that the nurse friend's seeming kindness to her was only veiled greed; she had seen her sit in her apartment eyeing the beautiful antique chair, the Indian rug she and Alfred had bought on their trip around the world— And so she gasped, kept gasping, her last into the receiver, having dialed O, and finally the call was placed, and they came and found her dead. Her nephew, by default, inherited all the objects that she'd had, and quickly sold them at an auction in the garage. Betty Henderson bought a small blue-flowered vase she had always liked and which once Gretta Grace had tried to give to her.

Claude was her hated nephew. He was, as it happened, my barber, or let us say hair stylist, at Mister Curly's of Dallas. That was the profession he had gone into, after flunking out of college, that she so much despised. So I had heard also of his aunt from Claude, who in turn hated her, but only quite objectively and bleakly. Claude was no mean hair stylist. I had known him when he was in college—he was nearly thirty now—and went to him, taking quite a bit of teasing from my family, as a lark, then kept going back as a luxury, liking very much the idea of having my hair cut so that it looked like it had not been cut at all. Claude had a private room with a black leather chair to put you in and a silk crimson cloth to put over you exposing just the challenge of your head above. He did very well at it, straight cut, razor cut, or styling, plus tips. Often—though not with me—he would pretend that he was foreign, being one of the few Dallas natives that I knew. He drove a bright red Volvo. He could command that coffee be brought and shoes be shined gratis for his regular customers. On his wall was

85

a color rendering of a fat-faced customer bald and then of this customer having been helped by a toupee Claude had designed and marketed. In the room next to him worked the boy he loved, who had a red leather chair and a bright yellow cape for customers. Claude was doing pretty well, no matter what his aunt might have thought.

But he was not happy.

He was terribly nervous. He had a tic in one eye and a slight spasm on one side of his mouth. It would jump and spasm when you looked at him, and it would jump seriously if you did not. Often his hands shook and trembled on your head; ministering to you the hands shook with the shears and clippers, trembling in fondling and caressing your head, patting every little hair in place. Often too he quarrelled with the others at Mister Curly's: with Essie when she swept his floor in a slovenly manner or did not bring the coffee hot or quick enough; with Sampson when he began a shine just before Claude was ready for the customer; with the other operators, and especially Jacques and Isidrio, who really were exotic, were foreigners, and who tried to intrigue the red-leather yellow boy next door. Claude hated them. Still his life seemed to go along and he had his place and his existence.

The last time I saw Claude was about a year or so ago, in the spring, about a year after his aunt died and he was running out of the extra good fortune of her money. (For she had been wise or clever enough to leave most of her actual money to a local foundation for the blind.) Claude was more nervous and trembling than I'd ever seen him that day.

I went into Mister Curly's of Dallas pressed for time and on impulse, without an appointment. I was getting ready to fly away somewhere and thought I'd take a chance. But Claude, they told me at the reception desk, was busy; I could not even be squeezed in if I waited. If I could wait, however, Isidrio could take me in a moment. I decided I could wait. One can usually wait.

I sat for a while in the reception parlor, gazing at the wall decorations and, furtively, at the other customers. Then Essie ushered me in to Isidrio, who still had another head working, a beatific young boy with closed eyes and long golden locks. Soon Isidrio had finished and flourished the boy out and I was up. No sooner, it seemed, had I settled myself in the cool blue relaxing chair than Claude came whipping into the room from his place across the hall.

"You have a good man there," he said to Isidrio. His eye twitched and his mouth was in contortion.

"Oh. Oh my. Is this your customer?" Isidrio said.

"Claude's my man," I said. "They told me you were completely booked up, Claude."

"Yes. I've been terribly busy. I'm sure Isidrio will take good care of you."

"Listen, can you work me in now?" I said.

Isidrio flipped the orange picador's cape back off me and I led Claude back into the black and red room and settled in his chair. He began to pat and clip my hair in silence, his hands shaking and trembling about my head like unfleshed clacking bones.

"How are you, Claude?" I said. "What's been going on?"

He stopped, paused behind me; then he went over into the corner, his back to me. Then he went and wrenched the hall curtain to our room shut. He looked at me. His spasmed face was in agony. He went back away from me and turned away, and then he began to sob and cry and shake all over. I sat dumbfounded with his scarlet cape over me and I think I asked him what in heaven was the matter. I thought the question, anyway. At any rate, he told me, crying, sobbing all the while. The boy he loved had left him, gone away, to California. I told him I was sorry to hear of it.

87

At that he did what I so ardently did not wish for him to do: he began to tell me, unleash, enumerate to me, all the miseries of his life. And he truly had a terrible life. I could say nothing, though; I did not want to hear of it. At the end he told me of a particularly horrid experience he had had the night before. (He was always having them, in terms of people.) But then he regained his composure, carefully washed and dried his face, carefully combed the oiled splendor of his black duck-billed block of hair, and came back behind me, cut my hair slowly and carefully, though they announced over the intercom that his next customer was waiting; and unpinned me from the chair and gave me my ticket and let me go. I pressed a dollar bill into his hand, now once more soft, limp, and professional. As I said, I never saw Claude again. He left and went to California, looking for his love, and I began to use Jacques, who is, to tell the truth, a better hair stylist.

The incident that had unnerved poor Claude the night before had taken place in a bar, a bar he had not tried before. He'd had some pills and also drunk too much, stingers or margaritas or some such, and at closing hour only the images before his eyes or in his mind were clear or alive in him. He had been asked to leave, by his waitress, clearing up around him. He was the only one there and had been asked to go. He had tried but could not seem to go; it was a blue and silver dark expensive bar. The waitress, a horrid woman twice as large as Claude, had come and picked him up by the shoulders and moved him, carried him, pushed him, handled him horribly and strongly, to the door and out into the night. She was a terrible woman, very tall with strange green piercing eyes and flaming red hair that fell to her shoulders. She was twice as strong as any man. He hated her and would always remember her. She had done violence to him. I did not, of course, tell Claude that I was pretty sure I knew the woman that he so vividly described.

I thought it must be Sally Smith.

She was big, and she could be rough, but she was also beautiful. She had told me that she was back working in a bar again. The great green eyes, the bright red hair, all that signalled to me Sally.

Sally Smith was a vital woman of many appetites and hopes. By now she must be forty-five, or maybe even fifty. It is very hard to tell a person's real age. She was of the earth earthy, like they say, but also smart. She was certainly the best secretary that I ever had. I hired her in spite of odd and spotty recommendations because of her sheer animal magnetism, her vitality, her great silked crossed legs putting all awry a short skirt when skirts were not so short, the wildness of her apocalyptic hair, the deep lost piercingness of her Mongol orbs, her large loose-mouthed scorning lovely grin at me— It challenged me as a man, and tried hard to forgive me for being one. That was true all the time she worked for me, several chaotic months, and of course I was half in love with her. Nothing, you understand, went on except her sheer presence near, around me, but I had the very deep feeling that I did not even want my wife to see her, filling up the little outer office next to mine. As a secretary she was precise and professional, much the best in our whole humdrum shop. But also scornful, straight-tongued, shafting all the myths and dull pretensions that prevailed among these women. So that all the other secretaries despised her. The president's and vice-president's girls would have liked to kill her, for she put a load of salt on them each day in her own aloof and animal way: saw them scornfully in terms of the mother fixes or shadow-sucking relationships they had to their bosses. And so they made up things about her, cruel, depraved things that went even beyond any reality.

Which was ironic: there was little need to make up anything about Sally.

Sally had been married seven times. When first I knew her she was recuperating from the last one but then another man, a garage mechanic, got after her. She did not even know whether under the Texas statutes it was legal for her to marry another time. Nor did I. She had a mess of children and was not sure where the various ones under various names had drifted to. She'd had no satisfaction from these men, these children, yet was hopeful that some day some way she would—find someone, something. She missed a lot of work days.

Finally, encouraged from above, that was why I fired her, not really wanting to. But she had borrowed money, not paid it back (though later it came to me, with one of her efficient pleasant notes); such a woman's moral character was of course in doubt; no employee should be allowed to miss so many days of work (even though she could come current with any needs and output in two days of effort in any given week); surely sooner or later she would seriously embarrass us, somehow blacken our good name by association if we kept her on. Okay, I said, okay.

Then, in the hot summertime, after she'd been out "sick" a week, it seemed to all of us, even me, that the game was up, the time had come. I was dispatched to have, in person, one of industry's patented "chats" with her; that is, to give her the ax, but of course as gently and sympathetically as possible, for we were nothing if not humane. Since she had no phone that was connected I went to see her, rather doubting that she would be there or even that the address we had would be correct. Upon advice and counsel I took a friend with me to this encounter. The friend was a minister buddy of mine, spotless in heart, mind, and deed. We pulled up to the crumbling apartment house on old McKinney that was the address we had and I asked him if he would not come along with me. He said he would prefer to stay sitting in the car at the curb. He was supposed to be right there with me so that she could not—what?—leap upon me with her great vital eyes, her wild hair, her Clytemnestra body, would not compromise me in any way. But I let him stay there; I suppose he could have come running if I had called, though actually we had no signal, no precise game plan worked out.

And I did find her in the apartment signified, a terribly cracked and disarrayed dull-green drab place. And with a man with her.

Now Sally looked about one hundred and eleven. She had been sick all right. She had, in that week, been operated upon twice for the female troubles that plagued her tortured insides, that periodically tore her open, stopped her in her quest for love, or whatever it was that was her quest. She had lost much blood, was thin, shaken, passive. The man was the garage mechanic who had been paying court to her. She had needed blood, and he had given blood to her, pints of it. He was a brown, thin, Indian-looking man with massive tattooed forearms. His name was Billy or some such. We shook hands, like two string-pulled figures in an old Chaplin film. Sally Smith sat at a cracked-linoleum–topped kitchen table smoking cigarettes. But she smiled and stood and put her hand out when I came in; she was glad to see me.

I explained that, good secretary that she was, she could not stay on with us. She simply smiled and said that it was all right. "I've had a hell of a time," she said. "But it's okay, sweetie. I'll bounce back in a day or two. Billy is taking care of me. Gee, darling, but I'm real sorry to have missed so much work. Gee, I hope I haven't embarrassed or upset you too much."

No, of course not, it was her not me I was concerned

91

about. I would be glad to give her any reference. Would I have a cup of coffee? Yes. Billy was the best strong black coffee-maker in the world, Dallas chapter of it anyway; he was a darling man. The fellow made the coffee, and we drank it, very sociably, with ritual and formality and, I trust, grace. As my collared buddy sat waiting outside in the car wondering what had happened to me, sweating profusely in the dog-day sun. But did not come up.

There was plenty of coffee, if he had.

Another Dimension

WHEN what's-his-name kicked off and left her with the kid, whose name she could never remember because He had named the baby-person, Sylvia thought she had better look for another dimension in her life.

She was only, you know, a decent, mature but not *old* age and He had stuck her out on the border between Richardson and the Turner Thesis, so the first thing she did was to move into a nice duplex in University Park so she could be near the university and culture and excitement and so the kid wouldn't have to, you know, have *problems* about going to school. That was not the sort of dimension she was looking for.

There wasn't much excitement there, though. She did almost get smashed or run over several times on Snider Plaza by elderly persons in possession of elderly autos, and one Sunday evening she stashed the kid and dressed scanty and sashayed over to the Tom Thumb in Old Town for a little casual shopping, which she had heard from her friend Ramona could be wildly exciting. Hang around the meat counter, and see what kind of meat the men buy, Ramona advised. Sylvia hung around the counter in her shorts and halter, and even though she was a little skinny, so a large dog could have taken her for his bone, she got a tumble from a distinguished-looking, gray-speckled, obviously still-virile man, just her type. (*He* had been fat and bald and that's a myth, about being bald, sister.) She observed him buying a stunning long and luscious tenderloin and coyly remarked upon it to him. He reddened up with pleasure at her remark and apologized prettily for having to hurry away to Check-Out in order to be on time to preach the evening service. Oh darn.

If she wanted to find it with a man, maybe she could find it at one of the gay swinging singles, or whatever it is, swingles, bars that, say, specialized in, ah, mature people, Ramona suggested. She, Ramona, would go with her. Sylvia said she was not interested in a *gay* bar. *Fun,* I meant, Ramona said. You had better get your language together, Sylvia said. She knew a thing or two about society and all. (She had always secretly suspected Him, in regard to, well, you know, *that.*)

Sylvia tried to tell Ramona that miniskirts and white boots were not the style anymore. She herself wore a simple surplice, without cowl. She felt a little awkward going to the Café Dallas, especially with Ramona. Ramona was a dear and a cool person and kept the kid for her a lot, but she'd had hepatitis real bad and had stayed a dingy yellow-ish in color and wore her hair a frizzy, funny way and light-ened it too much, so she looked like a fungoid peach. They lounged around the bar real casual and got a few looks, too, if you want to know, but no, what you might call, action. After about four hours Ramona, who turned out to be a big baby and a spoilsport, wanted to go home. The only thing that happened was that some toady-looking salesman type with a checked coat and striped pants dropped a motel room key in Sylvia's pocket as she came out of the john. The meat is always sweeter closer to the bone, or some such gallantry, he murmured to her, winking with the drunk eye that seemed to work. She dutifully mailed the key back to the motel.

Sylvia and Ramona went for coffee at Kip's, deciding they had certain standards.

It was time to turn to some cultural advantages. Sylvia went to plays and she went to an SMU piano recital that was pretty good but kind of eerie because only three other people were there. If the Symphony was having trouble it wasn't her fault. She went and sat up high at the back and shut her eyes and filled up with the music, and that was about the best thing she did. In those moments she felt it really was there somewhere; if she could just find something out there somewhere to attach her inside feelings to. She had a perfectly respectable degree in history or something from Iowa, and now she decided to upgrade her education and maybe meet some people in the process.

So she enrolled in an evening literature or something class at SMU and went there the first night full of perfume and high hopes. But there were thirty other women-people and just one man in the course, a fireman-person who was married and lived in Wills Point. After one class she heard a short plump divorcee go up to the professor and whisper to him she could tell that he was looking at *her* throughout the class. The professor assured her he was simply cross-eyed and God only knew who he was ever looking at. Well, it was a good try, the plump girl said. I'm divorced, you see, and . . . Of course, of course, said the prof, I understand, go read some Hemingway. Then he smiled at Sylvia and asked her did she enjoy *The Torrents of Spring?* She said she hadn't had any in a long time. He *was* cross-eyed, too, and wandered around the room a lot, looking for his thoughts.

Dallas is a pretty dead place, Ramona said. Maybe you should go some other places. I'll keep the kid. Ramona was staying in pretty much these days, having trouble with her color.

But before she set out for some more exotic place, Sylvia,

95

again on Ramona's advice, which by now was wearing a wee bit thin, made an appointment with the famous mystic and mind reader and prophesier Jerry Jeffy McBroom, just to see if her future could be smoked out, or if she *had* any. The ancient lady looked deep into her eyes and her skinny hand and traced the seven thoughtlines (*not* wrinkles) in her forehead and told her that she was going to meet a strange and wonderful man who would reveal a deep secret about life to her in a setting surrounded by vines and water. Sylvia couldn't wait, and set out to find him.

She went to San Francisco and then to L.A. and back through Denver and Colorado Springs and Estes Park, but he wasn't in any of those places, though everybody else was. Then she went to Taos, which she always had thought must be the most romantic, mystical place, and she sat looking out her motel window at the blue mountains and the gray-green valley and thought that there was plenty of dimension for somebody here but it didn't seem to sing to her soul especially, so she walked around Taos and this was summer and pretty hot and everybody who had been in California and Colorado was now walking around here in cameras and Bermuda shorts, so she had a cold beer.

Walking by the plaza something very strange wrapped up in a Penney's blanket lurched out at her from an alleyway and startled her so badly she shrieked and jumped a mile. It was an old Indian grinning at her, and there weren't any vines and certainly no water but she wondered if this wise old Indian didn't have some rare secret to tell her. Hi, he said, me Running Bear, you Little White Dove, no? You got thirty-five cents? You want go home with me? She gave him a quarter and watched as he sat on a bench in the plaza and spat at the tourists walking by. She took that for sort of a, you know, cross-cultural sign and went back to Dallas.

And Sylvia began to think she wasn't going to find it and

96

maybe she should get back in her bridge group and just face what her life really was and settle back down and watch her afternoon programs on TV. Come and grow old along with "The Edge of Night" and "The Price Is Right."

Then as luck would have it one day when she was just obliviously watching the fountain rise in the mall at North-Park she met a funny little man who was Lebanese or something and had little spindly legs and green eyes and huge forearms who was an osteopath and took her for coffee after they had admired the fountain together and confided he could help her with that slight curvature. She was excited beyond words when he called her for a date that weekend. They would go to a lake outside Dallas where a friend had a lake house and there would be a bunch of weird people there and they would eat and drink a lot and watch the boats go by. Remembering what Jerry Jeffy had predicted Sylvia thought that, after all, fate came wrapped up in odd packages, and while Georgie the osteopath was no prize just on the surface, maybe this was it. She accepted and he drove her that Saturday up to the lake in his Dodge van which he drove one-handed while she let him put his other paw on her knee, embarrassed only because it was so bony.

There were a bunch of weird people there, all right, of every nationality, and Georgie immediately got drunk and took out after a Rumanian beautician who looked pretty ripe, and that was the last she saw of him. They ate roast suckling pig and tomatoes and stuff from the host's garden, and the host was a huge old fat man who looked like Charles Laughton in a droopy bathing suit, and they drank and drank and drank cold cheap champagne and Rhine wine. He was the weirdest one of all and said she could call him Count Mippipopolous. She was pretty wise, having just had that course, and asked him, well, who does that make me?

He laughed and was very, you know, courtly, and carried a stick and wore a bush hat and kept opening the bottles. There were twenty sailboats with white sails out on the lake, which was very pretty, and then a little later there seemed to be twice that many with sails of all colors. Sylvia asked the count did he have a boat? Yes, just a small motor-boat down at the dock. His hostly duties prevented him from coming with her that moment but she was welcome to it, did she know how to run it? Of course, Sylvia had been in a boat before, when she was young. Well, my dear, be careful, for there is a current, and the wind keeps rising.

Clad in her sunbonnet, shorts, and halter, Sylvia walked (well, weaved) down to the dock and got tipsily into the little boat and pulled the cord and got the whoozis started and bumped three times into the dock and headed way out on the water, leaving all the revelry behind her. It was getting evening now. She turned the motor-thing up full speed and sailed over the water away from the sailboats and loved it going so fast all alone with the spray spuming over her. She thought, hell, what am I doing here, what am I doing in this life, and thought maybe she would just keep going.

She didn't see the stump she hit going full speed and then just rose up out of the boat as it hit the stump and kept on going and she came down in the water and was suddenly very much all alone out in the middle of the lake and it was dusk and she couldn't swim a lick and she really thought she'd found it then.

After she relaxed and didn't try to do anything but float she was okay though. Sylvia was still floating, her skinny body like a soaked twig, when it grew dark and then she even slept a little and when the early morning light came she was still floating and the waves had carried her in and there was the shore. So she stood up and walked in to the stony beach and here were some docks and houses and after she walked down the beach a while here was the count's dock and house. She sat on the beach in front of the fat old man's house for a while soaking up the early morning sun. It really was a beautiful early morning.

Then she walked up to the house and found Count Mippipopolous or whoever he was out in his bush hat and droopy trunks puttering around in his vegetable garden. Sorry about the boat, she said. Oh that is all right, he said, we cannot worry about such things. Maybe it will come back, he laughed. Here, you take this hose and water these tomato plants, and those cucumber vines. Cucumbers are delicious with white wine. What? Do it, my dear, this is very important, to keep it all living in this heat. He had another hose and was watering his adjacent roses. Sylvia stood there rather stupidly in her scanty outfit carefully watering the count's stuff. Vines and water. So?

So the count went and got two cane poles and put some pieces of leftover suckling pig on the hooks and motioned her to follow him down to the water. Some ferns were growing in the lake at the edge of the water, and now the lake was absolutely calm and waveless, an opaque sheet of glass. He threw his line out into the water, and she did the same. Neither cork bobbed once in an hour. Do you ever catch anything here, she said, I mean well, are there any *fish* in there? Oh no, he said, standing there fat and quiet, old eyes glued on his line and bobber. No, my dear, I really do not think so. After another hour or so of standing there with him fishing in the fishless lake she began to feel calm as anything, calmer even than she'd felt floating out on the lake at night when she expected to die.

99

In a while she looked at the strange old man and said, "This is ridiculous."

He shrugged and sighed and scratched his hairy belly. "Yes," he said. "Isn't it?"

Poet

BILLY BLAUBAUCH came to Dallas as a boy just out of a small Baptist college in West Texas. It was a nice little community there but it was too tight like his family ties were too tight and he had to get away. In Dallas he was at first known as the "boy copywriter." Others called him, though, a human candy apple and a magic prince and such. He did not care publicly. In his heart he cared. Billy Blaubauch had a heart as big and deep as the poor screwed world. In college he majored in music and beauty and now he went around with music flowing through him. At times he was homosexual but he was not always lonely. He came to Big D and was hired after waiting around forever by Haskerman Associates, advertising and p.r. Now that was seven years ago that he was a boy and nobody called him boy copywriter anymore and he hung in at Haskass where they let him stay lounging in a partitioned cubicle of his own for the simple reason that he was the best damn schlock copywriter in Dallas, and the quickest. Nobody could lunge at the typewriter and turn out the shit that would send the clients away grinnin' gigglin' and noddin' like Billy could.

But always he kept the vision of love in him and the music played in him. To them he was a Writer and he laughed at them. He knew he was a Poet. He knew it at night, alone, as he smoked a little pot in his apartment, his cell off the expressway, sensitive to all the human sounds through the paper walls of the hive all about him. He knew it but what true poet could afford to write a line? None, now. But God knew he was full of love, a poet who yearned to make art of the life around him.

In the mornings, as often as he could, he pulled up off his rack, coughed into coffee, had a Kool, and did the death-drive in to work. This morning the copy chief, hung-up girl, calling herself Ali Baba, she called a meeting, did indeedy. He slouched in with her and Hartman, owl all bespectacled, and Dumm Dumm and, smoking Kools, waited. Hasker-man was coming to address them. Ali Baba sneered at him. He rather liked her mustache. Dumm Dumm slouched over his pad, chewing on his stick. Hartman made faces for them. "Ha ha ha group, squirrel a bear-a-roo," he said. Hasker-man entered, moving in like a meddy ball being kicked by some foul foot. Looking at them he cut a wet, sly smile, let it ooze out over them.

"I will put it to you this way," he said. "We like to lost the Texas Gent thing. Why? Because you are not *work*ing. You have got your *fin*ger up your ass. You have got to get your ass off your feet. You think they make these goddamn things to sit in boxes in warehouses? Ali?"

"No, sir."

"This is a 1910 account. Client makes a long cheap cigar for men to suck on, stinks like hell, he should smoke it fishing, working in the yard. What's so hard? Skillern's has 'em six cents, a *val*ue. You got to be so goddamn cute. Cute cute *cute*. Client wants hard sell, you come tripping down the lane with a daisy in your ass. Right, Hartman?"

"Yes, sir."

"Okeh. So Billy here, he'll do it. Right? Give it the old pizzazz, hah, putzie?"

"Yes, sir," Billy said.

"The blind leading the blind," said Ali Baba.

"And the new account," Haskerman said. "Play with that."

The new account was for a male potency pill. Someone had named it Neutrino. It didn't matter, Haskerman said, that a neutrino has no charge, the market where they're going to sell it. It's anyway *a* plus *b,* male plus female. Result, nothing, said Ali. Hartman played with it all morning. Then he read:

"Neutrino, babies. A new Scientific discovery for Male Potency. Use just before intercourse to engender atomic fusion and/or fission of male and female atoms from your innermost depths to your lovin' solar system through chemical atomic interpenetration and interreaction—"

"Say there—"

"*Smart—*"

"This here Neutrino brushes away your peripheral electron belts and lets your sexual nuclei interact. *Millions* of positively charged electrons will be given off in the atomic structure of your love universe—"

Dumm Dumm beat his desk. Hartman was terribly pleased.

Ali Baba lay back in her metal chair, her legs thrust forth exposing hairy thighs, exclaiming, "Oh, Hartman! Hartman, lover!"

"Yes, yes, and do you know, he'll like it," Hartman said. He was from the East.

Billy Blaubauch deeply loved everyone but he hated Hartman and the girl and poor Dumm Dumm and Haskerman. He kept his Kool (five packs a day he smoked when all was well, and pot when not) and hit away at his precious keys, pecking, playing to the rhythms of the world in him. By noon he had, in re: Texas Gents:

103

```
            ACROSS AMERICA . . . CIGARS ARE COMING BACK
      TRAMP TRAMP TRAMP . . . SHE'LL LOVE YOU IF YOU SMOKE A
          LOVE                AFFECTIONATE
          BLOATING . . .          CIGAR COLIC
              MAR                 MMM
      ALLEGRO MAESTRO . . . CON BRIO . . . CAMERA OSCURA
          LONG CIGARS    SENTENCES   THOMAS WOLFE
      A GENERATION APART        LOST REGENERATION
              IMAGINATION          LOVE        APPLE
      APOPLEXY

                          PHLEBOTOMIZE
```

"God," Ali said, rising from her place, "I do need a change. Variety. It was such a beautiful day this morning. Did you see it? I have to do something, something terribly exciting—daring—different. I'll change bars."

But they went to lunch, as always, at Abe's, sat and chewed and then quit chewing and stared around them and at each other, smoking. Abe had bad breath and beans and chicken-fried. Dumm Dumm ate, hoggy, it was the only way he had to use his mouth.

They went to Hartman's very favorite place, the old dime arcade on Elm. Billy played nickel baseball with himself, winning five to three in two. But Hartman came and pulled him back to the high old wooden dirty machines. "*Listen* to him," he said, pushing him beside Dumm Dumm. Dumm Dumm made slight grunting sounds. Billy looked in the viewer with him. Scratchy jerky girl big round naval fat ass simpering back and forth a room jackaling your eye massaging medium breasts slowly slides down backasswards on motel bed running hands on all flesh writhing more to your big eye zooming in to snatch grinding grinning peeling down the pants *click*. Dumm Dumm put another dime in. Down the way Ali angled o'er otro machine.

After their creative lunch Billy Blaubauch and his friends were fatigued and did not much more that aft. Haskerman lunched at the Press Club liquidly an hour or three and did not come back. The Texas Gents, they sat them in the warehouses, long and cheap and stale.

In the evening Billy drank beer at Abe's. Everyone was there. Everyone was cute cute cute and had a lot of fun. Billy fell asleep with head on table and when he awoke the others were gone. He decided not to eat at Abe's. It was evening now. Something had to be going on. It was happening somewhere but he was almost always out of it. He went to Soul City or the In Crowd and felt the rhythms flow into him and he loved them all, they were so young, but it was the tragedy of Billy Blaubauch's life that he had been born fifteen years too early. All the young hippies lived on love, they were free and open like he wished to be. But he would just sit among them like a dunce, they did not even know he was there, so full of love and loving them. Billy smoked Kools till his fingers stank and his throat was raw with menthol. Often, sitting, Billy thought his throat had open holes in it and he was gorgeously dissolving. But he never took a trip, it would be bad for someone of his tendencies. Trips scared Billy.

There was a party somewhere. There had to be. Somewhere on Cole or Hall or McKinney or over by the school. Ali and Hartman were going somewhere. When he got there everyone was pretty gone. There wasn't any stuff, it was a heavy liquor bash. The booze was blistering off identities. Billy thought he would keep his and did not drink the hard. He had a ginger.

He hung self under Rouault clown in corner. Shriek of laughter. Jets kept blasting off. Noise noise noise. But he could shut it out, he had that trick. Image then was symphony of water and lovely ballet of people being ships, room a harbor full of ships of different tonnage, use, and grace. Continually upon bridge of each ship signal flags of exclamatory movements and expressions ran up and down. Ships changed places in the harbor, no aim or purpose, at will, or maybe a turned-on or faked-out harbor master somewhere. Hartman and Ali were there: black glasses and feline mustache. Yes: Owl and Pussycat. That was the central question: Dear Pig Are You Willing? Answer: yes yes yes. If you have blue head and green hands, sitting among them, full of love and ginger, no need for question. Foolish pre-answered question. Or green face, blue hands? Owl and Pussy-puss go upstairs on thick-carpet stairs, to pea-green boat? Dear Pig.

Looking, feeling sag, Billy saw Amazon, hair bleached blue, eyes green, huge, *cute* little skirt and massive massive legs on couch. Face like stone. She was a big mutha chunk of marble, leg-veins in marbly whorls. She put a large delicate hand like ice on Billy's little knee.

"I've been seeing you," she said.

Billy grinned a brilliant, foolish grin at her.

"I hate all these people."

"Surely not."

On his knee fingerbones arched like ice.

"See him? Big ball man? He wants me to sleep with him. They say he makes you do strange things."

"But you won't, will you?"

"Why won't? Tonight. Is why I'm here."

She snuggled out on couch, great white pins sprawling to the floor, head very heavy in Billy's lap. Ball man looked at them, Billy gave him finger, he went away. Billy could scare the big ones like him away. Dumm Dumm was lying on the floor doing contorted workings of his throat and mouth.

A very superior man there was a scientific research doctor who saw Billy nailed down and came over to dribble

106

drink on him and look down at him and explain his tremendously important scientific research.

"Can't you see," he said, "we have all these hot patients. Need is for cold cave to put them in. Right? Keep them down in there so can count them. Right? But it's murder. Can't get no good cold cement. See? I mean to build the cave to store the hot ones in to count them. *Verdad?* Counting babies now. Today counted big load hot rats hot dogs and a really hot primate."

"Nice. Sweet. Sweet sweet sweet."

"You damnfool. Don't get it. Count the count! See? How totally can you get them hot? For science, health. If you had a tumor eating you, how cold could you get? Lay you out on plastic tray, on plain pipe racks—"

"I know you now," Billy said. "Know you well."

He bounced the girl and Bobby Hall the science man, and entered night, looking for the real.

Gorgeous. It was gorgeous, Bach-night. Moon a scimitar. Stars sprinkling the black. It was a sign of the perfection of the plan of the world and universe and you could equate yourself with it, if you were a poet. If you were a dumb-ass poet playing at objective correlatives. Billy Blaubauch could not do that. He had enough irony and pity, oh he was full of love and irony and pity, he just was not that kind of poet. He was a poet though. There was a poem in him, he could not both live and utter it, great poem always symphonizing inside wanting to get out. He was full of a lovely vision of the world.

So like poets do he walked the park under the dark, by the statue of General Lee. Now General Lee, he had been well reared. There were, sir, mosses on the old marse. I am a Southern boy myself, now a creator of harmless gainful images, like yourself. Small correction though: m'folks fought for Union. Scab Krauts. Houston men. Went to Cin-

cinnati, fought *mit* Sigel. Then came back. Very popular. Indeedy. He, Billy, should have stayed, run a store. But tight,
too tight. No loitering here, young traitor. The pigeons they
will shit on you as me. Bug off, pigeon: take your mule
and gun.

Now Billy in the park came upon three trees and two
benches, a lamp post. On one bench sat a man running his
hands over the smooth belly of a guitar. Billy sat down on
otro bench, by a small old lady.

"Do you have another cigarette, sir?" she said.

"Oh yes. Yes yes. Yes indeed. But: A Kool."

She nodded all righty, he gave it to her. He did light it for
her and she puffed with pleasure, holding the whited weed
out from her at old-lady angle.

"Thank you," she said. "Very much. Now pleasures are
so few. I must admit cigarette smoking has come to be a
major one of them. I had a whole pack at the beginning of
the week—do you remember when the week began, so
long ago?—but I have started doing the *worst* thing—I
smoke a whole cig instead of cutting them half in two. You
can't imagine what it does to my budget. My goodness, isn't
it interesting what they are learning about cigarettes?"

By them the man plucked a chord, a minor chord. Billy
Blaubauch saw that it was the Owl, red glasses shining
under yellow lamplight, image-wise.

She continued to smoke, with antique relish.

"Oh my," she said, "I can imagine what my children
would say—if they knew I had taken to smoking! They
have no idea, you see. When I see them, what a surprise it
will be. I have not seen them for eight years. But my grand-
son writes. Quite regularly. I do fine. Oh my. I have a good
life, young man. Yes yes indeed. What I want you to know
is that my life is full."

Billy realized then that this was his grandmother. She was up in Iowa. He should have recognized her before. He wanted to embrace her but just sat there by her.

"I'm taking the nicest course now," she said. "It's the Romantic Movement, you know. All the Romantic poets died so young. I only pay ten dollars for the whole two-month course, it is what is called a short course. The sweetest young man teaches it. We're on Wordsworth now. It's so lovely."

"Why don't you sing?" Billy shouted at the Owl. Sometimes he could not stand all the music and no singing.

He stopped running, skying, through the park, hurtling down the hill as a blind man tapped toward him.

"How do you do?" quoth the man. "How do you do do do? I trust someone is here. I thought I was being called. I thought I heard old music that I know. Who are you, sir? Identify yourself!"

In terror of love Billy said: "Your son, sir. Your goddamn sorry son."

"Ah! I have nothing to say to you. Have you read, why don't you read, why don't you read, my volume on logic, boy? It is out of print, the print is out of it. Listen: this is all I have to say to you:

"Ah! Darkness! Horror of darkness unfolding, resistless, unspeakable visitant sped by ill wind in haste!

"Dark eyes, now in the days to come look on forbidden faces, baby, do not recognize those whom you long for—"

"Hear hear," someone said. "Hear hear hear hear." A chorus of many small men in sightless shades laughed behind him, laughed him out of the park to home.

Home was where the pot was. But up the narrow stairway, foot-scraped green, Billy stopped at a door across from his. French and Swann were here, he knew them not but saw them much, coming up and going down, coming in and going out. In two different ways: in cocked cap and uniform of red, blue, and gold, a-jet o de-jet, or Sunday morns, kid, in the hallway by this door clad loosely in flaming wrappers bending to pick up Dallas *News* or *Herald.* Yea. He did not know which was French and which was Swann. He imagined French more cavalier, the redhead one, disdaining to clutch wrapper as she bends, titties jumbled cattywhomp. Swann more ethereal then, kneels, clutching neck though wrapped all quite in sheer. Diaphanous. Indeedy. What did they do? Smile at him but never bother. Never party. Come and go, come and go, talking of whatthehellio, never disturbing, evenings, his dippings in Goethe-boy. Would they would. Billy had intention some day of buying them each a book of Proust in the liquid tongue and leave them these one Sunday here at this door. Ethereal kid got to have *Swann's Way,* of course, but French, at odd moments he thought he'd like to have *Within a Budding Grove.* Unless Swann were French, and French was Swann.

Being level, standing level like a cool moon, on odd impulse, Billy knocked the door.

Upon its act of opening he looked and saw a sharp full face of white, saw small breasts of venous white, red buds set on surrounding zones of faintest brown and when she smiled and nodded him in and turned and let him in the room, immaculate cushions of surprising scope and softness and when she turned again pointing him to a chair, the small and elegant protuberance of softest fur. They sat.

"Do you be Swann?"

"Nah—" Voice Yankee, Kansas-like. "French. Swann's in there. What do you do?"

"Images. I am an image monger."

"Beautiful," she said.

In came Swann, the solid Swann. In uniform. She looked at him.

"Tell her," Billy said to French, "I'll take her. I'll take French to Love."

"Swann, baby."

"Come on," she said, "take Swann baby to the planes."

He took her out Mockingbird to Love. She talked Chicago to him but he liked her best and he wanted to be up over it all and look down when the new day came and bestow a benedict on them all. He wanted big mutha Swann to sneak him on.

She sneaked him on the plane. It was big and silver. She led him up the thing past them all and in the tourist and told him to lock self in the lav till flight.

He stayed there for long long time, or else it stopped. Billy Blaubauch never used a watch. He began to smoke and groove and talk back to the place: "Please do not put metal or glass objects, cloth or debris in toilet." All righty. "Ask stewardess for electric shaver." No need, someone'd left old rusty razoo lying here in sink. For him? Gift of Swann? The place began to bother Billy really. There was a slot on wall, like a mail slot, under which was writ: *Return to Cabin*. What did it mean? Was it an appeal to him as a poet? He found self out of Kools. He felt foolish, light-brained. Could Billy Blaubauch squeeze self into small enough ball to shove him through the slot? What would they do if he returned self to cabin? He hated hideous impossible slot.

Suddenly roar began and roaring came and plane began to shudder and Billy thought he heard him scream, looked at image of him in the glass. Taxiing, he held on to the sink where was sick unto. Then, shuddering quivering mightily and highly noise noise noise he found the vision. Once again he saw his vision. He was a poet, yes, full of love, must get it out. As the thing shook and began to blast fast ahead he fell forward over sink, slashed self with razoo and began wildly to write his poem of love in mirror, in blood, but lift-off dragged him back to crash in foolish heap down under slot and Billy never, never came back from the trip.

The Antichrist

KARL WOLFGANG WENDLAND.

It was a name that brought me pleasure, and then suddenly seemed the most sinister that I had ever known.

Now it seems to me more sad than sinister, but terrible still.

The year I am recalling is 1952. I was a new graduate student then, doing Master's work in English at the university here, a Teaching Fellow, taking three courses and teaching two freshman classes, teaching in the mornings, boot grammar by negative example, often reading from the textbook in desperation when hung up on the use of the gerund as an adverb or some such thing, pacing the classroom, staring out the window at the still campus, then in the afternoons trying to sell pharmaceuticals about which I knew nothing but the Latin names I memorized to doctors I never got to see, and in the evenings throwing a paper route, being yelled at because the paper was delivered late, or cursed because often it was not folded correctly and would open as I threw it and sail in several flapping sections into the waiting yards.

It was a confused and crucial and beautiful young year, when I was poor and idealistic and just married, and I was living under several influences.

One was Eich. One was Milo. The other was Karl Wendland.

113

Milo was the one whose spell I was most under, because I truly loved him.

Milo was a teacher. No advanced degrees, a weary peripatetic who had taught freshman courses here or there for many years, a ruined, defeated old teacher, Milo was, for all his satiric shield and timeworn oblique edges of personality, yet sweetly spirited. Who loved to teach those damn kids, to read and mark and form their ragged themes. (*Old?* My God, who was then about the age that I am now.)

Milo, who had, who never had any more than, the rank of instructor, was my officemate in the basement of the old building. Sometimes he would suffer me, and we would talk.

And Eich. He was critical, cynical, objective, a brilliant mind, a scholar. His study was of the structure and history of the language, but sometimes he would relax and teach Shakespeare, making of the plays a pattern of neologisms and syntax, a scholar's code, relieving them of their humanness, their glory. I despised Eich, and feared him. I thought that he was almost evil, that he stood for the dead hand upon life and literature, in comparison to Milo, who loved the merest essay that he taught, if it had any worth at all, and made you love it too.

And Wendland. How shall I describe Wendland and what he meant to me, and then came to mean to me?

Eich wished for me, for all of us who were the department's slaves, its Fellows, to go on and take the Ph.D., a good Ph.D. somewhere reputable, and never to return to his university, but to bring honor to the department. His family had been killed in Germany.

Wendland gave a piece of silver to my wife and me when we married. He had us, with other students, out to his farm in the evening to roast franks and drink cider around a fire, when he sang to us Middle English ballads.

He was in his sixties. Tall, white-haired, ruddy, a splendid-looking man, but somewhat shambling in his gait. He carried a stick and wore a pith helmet as he walked to and from his house nearby to the campus, and his little dog accompanied him. For forty years Karl Wendland had taught in the university. It was legend that he was, early, one of the best and most popular teachers. It was said that he'd taught *Beowulf* to standing-room classes of sixty or seventy students. I knew that he had written books. You could find him in *Who's Who* and in the *Dictionary of International Scholars*. He had done definitive work on the Finnsburg Fragment, and then had turned to a series of pleasant little works for children on the tribes who held England in the days of Alfred. His was a distinguished name in Anglo-Saxon.

And he was Ph.D., Johns Hopkins, and B.A., Oxon., and of an old family of southern aristocracy.

All of which, I am sure, contributed.

I remember so well the pleasure of my first class in Old English with him.

Together we chanted the Lord's Prayer in Anglo-Saxon.

Then: "How do you pronounce this word?" he said, writing O-h-t-h-e-r-e on the blackboard.

I raised my hand, having studied in advance alone the old language, relishing it.

"Oht-here," I said.

His blue eyes, the yellow-white mustache, crinkled with pleasure over the rich red lips. "Only one other student has ever got that right," he said. "Most are not aware, and pronounce it with the *th* sound. You will do well, my boy, you will do well."

After class he called me up, and congratulated me again, and asked my name, and if I was Jewish, which I thought a little strange.

And I did do well, and enjoyed him and his class thoroughly, though others seemed somewhat cowed in there. I told some other students that Karl Wendland was the best teacher I'd ever had, much more alive and spirited than Eich, under whom I was reducing the history of the language to formulae. They seemed to think that I was crazy, but not many people liked Old English, its difficulty, much.

Milo it was who told me what I should have found out, should have known. He had taken to coffee once or twice a beautiful young senior student named Sally Cohn. I came into our office when she was there and saw that she had been crying, and she looked at me and left.

"The old bastard," Milo said. "The damnable old bastard. Made her stand up in class, in the middle of his Renaissance class, and admit that she was Jewish."

I sat down, dumping my load of unmarked themes.

"Oh, she admitted it all right," Milo said, smoking his cigarette savagely. "She made public confession of the fact. It would not be a bad idea for me to get up from here and go up into that evil stinking office of his and kill him. That, I suppose, is the only remedy for him."

Milo, the old seeming-apathetic stoic.

"What?" I said. "Wendland? What?"

"Go read that book he inscribed for you so beautifully," Milo said. "You stupid little horse's ass."

Karl Wendland had presented me with a copy of his latest book a few days before. Its odd title was *The Wall around America*. With a plain cover, privately printed, it had seemed to be something out of his field, perhaps even political, but I had been busy and had not gone into it, not taken it beyond the title page. There he'd written, in his elegant script, "To a brilliant young linguist. *Ad astra!*"

And I went and read the book then, read through it in one searing night of reading.

At first I could not believe what I was reading; but then I came to believe it all too well.

Essentially Professor Wendland held the idea, presented in the book, that all Jews were communists and all communists were Jews.

It was a very neat idea, and it framed all his view of history, and of the present situation in our nation and the world. Jews were identified with the Eastern hordes. The greatest moment in history came with the halting of the advance of these hordes at the Elbe by the Teutonic Knights. But their insidious inroads had perverted the cross of Christ and the destiny of Western Christian man ever since. For Jews, you see, were in secret control of all the nations of the world, and ever had been, since that early noble, courageous time. Secretly, using a veil of anti-Semitism over the minds of the peasant masses, Jews in the Comintern ran Russia. Oriental Jews were in control in China. As for America, Wilson's advisor Colonel House, whom Wendland once had met, was a Jew, and in control throughout Wilson's term, through his sickness and his phony internationalism and his leading us on the secret course to war. It was no secret that Franklin Delano Roosevelt was a Jew, and an ally of the Reds. Now, Eisenhower was a Jew.

Thus, with Jews in control of all the nations, and all wealth, and all power of the world, all wars were waged for their profit, nations rose and fell to their benefit. America was completely surrounded, and rotten at the core. But there were still good Christians in America, still some who could and would rise to fight the Red Jewish menace and save America.

These, I supposed, comprised those who had already taken Dr. Wendland's book into its seventh printing.

"And do you see that the bastard has dedicated this last edition, the one you have, so proudly signed, to the B'nai B'rith," Milo said, "without whose interest, as he says, its success would not have been possible? Jesus God!"

"That's it exactly," Milo said as we talked of it again, when my dismay had begun to turn into the coldest kind of anger. "The worst thing about it— Oh hell, boy, bigots abound, always will, I reckon, skunks smelling their own odor and callin' it bad— But what this man has done, lent his name as a scholar, his reputation, to this fabrication of genius—genius because there is just enough truth in it, enough facts—an actual battle here, a historically valid judgment there—to make the straw into the phony brick to make the construct, and to give credence to it in the eyes of the stupid and the ignorant. That's a *sin,* boy," Milo said. "For a teacher, a scholar, that is a terrible sin. To say nothing of the basic hatefulness of it, the sickness of the man."

And that is what I did: say nothing.

But I went to class sparingly, only just as much as I calculated could let me keep my A. He knew, of course. I could tell it from his smile at me, which in a darting, nearly maniac way if you began so to interpret it, was really very merry. And I begrudged and berated myself the times when he taught well, moved me and the class to an appreciation of the old language—the saga of the slaying of the monsters. And hated myself when something in me could not help but respond to the magnetism of the man, his vitality, his zest. My God, what vital force is it that evil has, that we pale before it?

I began to join those who knew who slunk down the hall to the classrooms by his large office lined with books and dusty portraits of Jespersen and God knows who else where his secretary—the only private secretary in the department—sat like a black-iron stove sorting, filing, never smiling, a Mrs. Woodcipher, and where he would be, laughing jollily, with men in dark shirts and brown ties with floppy hats they did not remove. I remember so clearly the seamed set faces of those men as they sat in there, as if drawn into some sort of absurd cartoon.

And the semester went on. Wendland wrote, and distributed, to us, to the town, and beyond, a pamphlet pointing out how our university was in the hands of the communist Jewish conspiracy and quite out of the hands of the church from whose womb it had not too long before tottered.

Everyone knew, then.

"He is the Antichrist, the very Antichrist!" our president, a handsome, athletic young man, said to me on campus one day. "Do you know what he said to me? He *smiled* at me and said—he *smiled* at me—'Who's going to bell the cat?'"

"Well, I'm glad we're smart enough not to do it," Milo said. "I'm glad we ain't going to grant him martyrdom."

"Shit," Milo said, "that would take it into twenty printings."

And in November, late, young MacDowell, of History, petitioned for a called meeting of the General Faculty, and got enough votes to call it, declaring he would offer a motion of faculty censure of Dr. Karl Wolfgang Wendland.

I was talking about my term paper in linguistics with Eich, and abruptly asked him what he thought of this.

For a moment I did not think that he would answer me, wondered if I had disappeared for my presumption. His cold eyes stared away from me, his ice-like face held in one bony hand. Then he answered, spitting as he spoke, speaking to me a speech.

"I have hated every fascist thing he has ever done, said, or written. For thirty years.

"And yet, much as I favor, emotionally, Dr. MacDowell's motion, as odious as he is to me, I refuse to vote to censure him.

"I have fought him—and finally just avoided him—in this department. He has made my life hell. He has severely damaged the reputation of this department which I—and I must say this, which he too—labored to build over the years.

"But strictly speaking, and no matter what—no matter what in *hell*—they are, he has the right to hold to his opinions.

"Have you found that he presents these opinions to you in his class?"

"No. But he—"

"What?"

"Never mind," I said. His cold eyes looked at me, and I could have read more mercy or humanity in a snake's. Were these the eyes of justice? I could not feel so . . .

Yet, my own eyes said into them, they killed your people, man!

Do not presume to say another word to me, they glittered. *I have relish in this: My only pleasure is to hold the ark in my hands and smell of it, that it stinks.*

So I went away from him, my idea of writing my paper on international languages having been rejected.

And in early December the faculty held its meeting.

MacDowell moved his resolution of censure.

Milo got up and left the meeting.

The vote was 351–1 to censure Wendland. I voted against him. Eich cast the only dissenting vote to the resolution. That day I stayed late in my basement office (Milo off somewhere, I imagined drunk), grading themes. Walking home along the edge of campus I encountered Wendland, going along with his little dog, and his hat, and stick. The sky was gray and the sun had a peculiar orange light to it not common to the prairie. He was going along laughing, talking to himself, shuffling almost into a dance. He grabbed my arm as I nodded, before I could dart by. He looked at me with great good humor and forgiveness. He leaned his ruddy red face into mine and the bright blue eyes caught mine straight on for a moment: "The only thing I fear," he said, "is an assassin's bullet." And caned forward, walking like a bear, following a new route toward home, the little dog sniffing the way before him along the trail, warily, warily.

The censure bothered him about that much. The book had more printings. The university let him teach until retirement.

Eich, I understand, died a few years ago. Milo is still teaching somewhere. Soon after all this I left graduate school and went into advertising.

In retirement Wendland wrote a very pleasant novel of his childhood and had it privately printed. Wendland died finally, neither admired nor feared nor much remembered by anyone. Which was in my mind just now as I took from the shelf and balanced in my hands my inscribed copy of his book.

Pot

JOSEPH WARD RED-BIRD was an Indian Quaker pacifist. After taking his Ph.D. in chemistry from Yale he became increasingly aware of how man was polluting his world, and of man's other inhumanities. He went to Mexico and began to dig in certain ruins there, taking a certificate in anthropology. Then he went to Berkeley and added, in just two years, a second doctorate in social engineering. There he met and married Anna Martinson, a great tall blonde laughing-eyed girl—a missionary of the church as radically reformed—who hailed from New Zealand. He was very grave and gentle, she very kind and loving, enthusiastic. In the late sixties he accepted a teaching position and the newlyweds moved to Dallas. They settled in a large decaying house on Swiss Avenue and often in the evenings they could be seen walking arm in arm under the large old trees. Blushingly Anna would admit that they recited poetry to each other walking; hers was her own. At night Volkswagens and Saabs and old Fords with stickers on the bumpers would come and park in front of the house and the lights behind the curtains would go on and stay on long into the night. Soon the old mansion on Swiss came to be called by many in the city the Peace House.

I thought that Joseph Redbird and his lovely wife were remarkable and I thought the old house remarkable too.

Downstairs the old maroon-hung living room, with fireplace, was used for meetings with Joseph's students, for meetings of the Dallas Peace Association, for many other gatherings of gentle or intellectual and cause-moved people, or just, in my case, for tea with the Redbirds, the dark hot tea with lots of cream and sugar or lemon in the heavy stoneware cups. Around the room were strewn the research and writings-in-progress of each of the Redbirds, the Oklahoma boy and the New Zealand girl who was applying for citizenship, and it was perfectly safe there, no one ever violated it by touch or glance, because it was important to them. Each wrote for a certain set of journals, so that we knew that this work was important beyond them, and us, too. Each wrote well, and with the fire and gentleness of an old humanist tradition. They eschewed the "society" of the town, which tried to capture them a time or two, and made this room, and the place where Joseph and I taught, the center of their lives. Joseph brought to our university the first truly interesting and significant film series that we had ever had. Joseph was fascinated with the medium of film, from Chaplin to Bergman, and with the nature of reality, about which he was to learn something during his stay in Dallas.

The other large downstairs room housed, on shelves Joseph had sawed and hung, an excellent library in politics, history, sociology, and literature, several hundred of Joseph's books, including the most complete collection on Vietnam I'd ever seen. These books were loaned to whoever of the people who came in and out of the house might be interested in reading them. You simply signed them out, and almost all of them came back.

A small basement room of the house was donated as the editorial office of an "underground" newspaper called the *Dallas Daily Bread.* I knew the young editor and talked to him there. The paper had been banned from my university, where it had been started, and I had spoken for it then, according to the notion of the free dissemination of ideas which I held.

Out back, beyond the old abandoned greenhouse around which Anna tried to grow a few shrubs and flowers, they let a gentle person rent the run-down garage apartment.

These were the two mistakes they made, along with the views they held and advocated anyway, in regard to the perfidy of the war and the injustices in society.

Early on Joseph began to be hassled, because of his dark Indian looks and his thick black hair, and because of the "foreign" license plate on his old Volvo, and because of the blue peace symbol superimposed on the flag on a sticker on his car, and the green ecology decal on the car's window. Several times in that old neighborhood of Dallas, at night, for no real reason, Joseph would be stopped in his car, flashlight shined in his face, license checked. He laughed about it, but of course it bothered him. "Well," he smiled, "pretty soon they should get to know me."

And, as he, and Anna, continued to write and teach, and rap with people, and provide a home for the harassed *Daily Bread,* and speak at peace meetings at the Unitarian Church and in the parks, I am afraid they did "get to know" him.

Joseph and I were both teaching a course we had conceived for senior students called 20th-Century Issues. Its purpose was to prepare our students to be thoughtful citizens, to see themselves and the careers they would soon embark on in a larger context, to make valid decisions in a troubled time. Joseph had a fierce belief in the possibility of a democratic system of government, in its checks and balances, the system which had been one of man's great experiments, which counts so heavily on the participation of the knowledgeable individual, and which is bending under immense pressures now, and going awry. One afternoon of the second term he met me in the hallway as I was going into class.

"Anna and I have been arrested for possession of marijuana," he said. "We've posted bond. I assure you, it's a false charge. I have been extremely careful about that. Whatever it was they found, it wasn't ours. We don't use the stuff."

I said that I believed him, as I did. I agreed to write a letter of character reference for him. His departmental chairman and others also did this; the university stood with him. The only thing that truly bothered him, he said, was that Anna was deeply upset. She did not at first believe that it could happen, and then it frightened her. The police had come in upon her abruptly, showing her a tiny plastic pot from her backyard with a sprig of something in it, asking her was it hers?

We heard about it that night on local television news, judge and jury: *Professor found growing grass in greenhouse.*

Later they called one night, and then came by. Anna brought a lovely yellow candle to us, and I had a small bottle of Cabernet, and we talked and drank it and watched the candle flicker.

Their lawyer was a minorities-rights lawyer who worked skillfully for them. The morning that the matter went before the Grand Jury we drove downtown to meet Anna and Joseph in the courthouse, to wait and drink coffee with them. Joseph went in briefly to appear. In a while the lawyer came to tell us they had been no-billed. I was delighted, thinking at least justice had been done, absurdity had not triumphed. But Anna said: "It doesn't matter. I can never live in this place now." For the rest of the term they moved out of the Peace House into a small apartment near the university, had to do with almost no one, finished up their tasks and responsibilities.

"It can happen again," she said. "How can we think it won't? One cannot live like a clam, looking over one's shoulder all the time. My Lord, my father is an official in the hinterland of New Zealand, and I've never seen anything happen like this before." And though he very much, he said, enjoyed the work he was doing here professionally, Joseph resigned. Some time later he accepted a position in Canada. Later yet some sort of an intelligence officer came to question me about the Redbirds, and I was courteous to him in my office.

The last time we saw them was at a small gathering we did not enjoy. A woman was there who had burned a flag in protest of the war. Her bitterness dominated the conversation. She and her husband and children were moving to Mexico because of the repression here. She had been through an awful lot, and her position was understandable. The Redbirds did not say much, and somehow I was uneasy about the woman as a foil for them at this moment. At any rate, we said goodbye and saw them last there with her.

Anna and Joseph are now both still teaching in Canada. They have a child. Years go by, but when we think of it, we correspond.

The Horror

THE phrase came to her as a vague, almost meaning-less incantation as she stood in the small den where his bookshelves were, no one else of the party celebrating "the great Paul," "the cultural conscience of Dallas," in the richly jacketed little room but her constant companion, Worm. A phrase vague and out of context, like "oh my God" or "what the hell," the kind of neutral phrase one might utter at the final stroke or as the penultimate pain pierced chest or arm.

Now she stood with her jeweled hand with its blue raised veins, looking to her like the too white skin of a rare snake, on the strangely tattered little Modern Library volume with the story in it. She had always admired the technical view-point in the story and abhorred the story itself but loved Joseph Conrad. *There* was a man I could have loved with passion, she had told Henry. Henry had nodded, being just an oilman and not a writer and by then well used to the fate of being her husband, used to allowing her her way, used to his role of colorless squire at her publishers' parties in New York and Dallas. She'd told him by then she could have loved with passion also Flaubert, Tolstoy, who else? Proust? he'd asked slyly. Henry James? With malice. Now Henry was moaning and moldering in his grave and she missed him, in her way. He had cared for her, protected her, so well in *his* odd, tentative, trusting, Texas way. It seemed a horrible weight of decision whether to pull out the little book from the shelf. There was another story in it that she liked: "Miss Brill." The young couple in the park had laughed at Miss Brill, upset her romantic world of fantasy, and *that* day she had *not* bought the little slice of cake with an almond in it but had gone home and hung her old fur, that looked to the cruel young couple like a fried whiting, in her closet, and thought she heard crying coming from it . . .

Well, she was no Miss Brill. It was just that it had become harder in some moments to be, or to know, who she was, so much harder than before. She had been so beautiful as a girl. At college in the East she had loved being the Texas beauty. She could have married or had affairs with many men. Instead she'd had them in her mind, put them in her books, and had the certainty of Henry. "The great Paul" had praised her in his columns through the many years, book by book. But now there was no book. As a girl she'd had a pony.

Worm, her current sycophant, kept filling her wineglass. He wanted her money, of course. Her secret was that there was little money left, most of what she had gleamed dully on her wrists, on her fingers, lay over her powdered breast. It was, she thought, still a magnificent breast, a hell of a nice pair for a woman of her age, yet unshrunken. It was her heart which shrank. She heard the chatter of leave-taking in the living room beyond, with its deep blue and orangish Oriental rugs. Her host, the one honoring the "cultural conscience," whose books these were, she had first thought also wanted her money, to endow himself. Tonight she had realized that was not so, or true no longer. His attitude had changed. He had hardly acknowledged her presence here tonight. Since the failure of his imagination, the cessation of his writing of poetry and fiction, since his turn to criticism, he had, she thought, become slimmer, aloof, half-blind; his heart had hollowed and grown cold, he seemed to despise her own dearly paid-for talent.

She'd had everything, wealth, beauty, intelligence, she hadn't *needed* to be doggedly true to her damn Muse all these terrible years, couldn't he see that? He had grown perfectly cold and indifferent to her, for which she bleakly despised *him*. So there, you bastard.

Worm slid out of the little room as she turned a piercing gaze on him from eyes so dark they were nearly black, both retinas reattached. She opened up the bastard's book, to the damn story: "It was curious to see his mingled eagerness and reluctance to speak of Kurtz. The man filled his life, occupied his thoughts, swayed his emotions." She'd left fiction after that first novel, that *cause célèbre*. It had stood Dallas on its Philistine ear. She'd never known whether Henry really thought . . . After that, she'd fastened onto her subjects like a leech, bleeding them for truth . . .

A few minutes before, just before she had come in here, "the great Paul" had finished his peroration. He had been at his best, dear boy; arranged them in a circle around him, spoken endlessly, with wit and anecdote, of *personages,* of every editor and author who'd ever come to this damn Prairie Parnassus. Oh, he had been *charming*. His swan song. It had made her feel Proustian and horrible. He had been charming, true to all he'd ever said or written or believed, which was unforgivable; and he had grown to be seventy, and his death was in him, and she felt Proustian like Marcel coming out and down into the room among his former friends and they were all in costume, in masks: white-haired, shrunken, withered, *old*. She had seen Jason's *skull* behind his mask as he stood, half smiling, listening to Paul.

Their host had collected all of them together for this affair. As some respectful, macabre joke? Luther's wife had hissed, "It's *Luther* who is the great man here!"

She pushed the tattered little book of stories back upon its shelf. She had turned to writing biography then, of men, then of their women, then, making her way, of women. Oh, she had known, felt in her bones, what was now in the air, known it long before the punk sisters knew it, felt it, feared and fought it . . . She placed her fingers on a volume of the late James as her host came in the room. She'd seen the horrible place where James had died, in Chelsea, looking to the coldly turgid Thames. He'd gone a little crazy at the end and thought he lay in the old beauty of Lamb House, at Rye.

Women, you cold, critical, heartless bastard, live it, feel it, know it finally, too—

"I believe we share an affinity for James," he said.

She turned and set her glass down on his shelf and looked at him with scorn. She turned her handsome head and coiffed mane—all her own hair still, you puppy—and withered his shelves with her glance. The James, the Proust, the Flaubert he had made just a short shelf. He had no taste, really. He'd kept all the books he'd apishly reviewed. Their jackets made, really, a discord, a cacophony of distraught, undefined colors: Kerouac, my God, and *Howl,* that madness, to his weak nostalgia for a mythologized Texas to *Future Shock.* All the detritus of four decades now she had neither loved nor understood.

"Do you like Ford Madox Ford?" he said, still cruelly.

"Would you get my wrap?" she said to him.

There was a mirror over the mantel in the living room, where Paul sat drinking black-labeled whiskey like a throwback, still talking, the swan its last moment on the thinning waves of air before the deep descent, with dear kind Jason, his hawk's eyes unblinking in his skull, and Luther, potted, in the circle listening, still listening to Paul. The Heirs of Apollo, of Pollo, she thought: her little joke. Worm looked up and smiled his fop's smile at her and made to rise to join her but she waved him down, imperiously. She did not look at the gilt mirror. The bastard of course would have such a mirror. Henry, of all authors, had loved Mark Twain. She had not told Henry, in the talks she still had with him now, that it had come to funny old Mark Twain too, the *horror*. It would be cruel to tell Henry that— She did not look at the mirror as she passed, she did not wish to see her face. She knew that face, how it would appear, the smear of lines of life and such hard work upon it now collapsing . . .

She smiled brilliantly at her host as he let her out his cold front door, her fur like a fried whiting wrapped around her, covering her breasts, her body, her diamonds and her sapphire.

"Such a lovely party," she said to him. "My grandfather, who traveled a great deal abroad, once met Joseph Conrad, in London, when Conrad had just come off the sea and hardly knew English."

He smiled and carefully closed the door.

She smiled bleakly back at the door. She looked up and saw a star, and by habit began to make a pattern, until she felt dizzy seeing stars, blackness.

She grasped tight the pony's mane, turned and stepped down, into the void.

Whatever Happened to Danny McBride?

"WHATEVER happened to Danny McBride?"

I was rereading Erasmus, who sought to unite faith and knowledge. "The Godly Feast." As he said of the prideful, "They embraced the shadows and neglected the substance." As his friend Timothy, having come to dine and discourse with him, said, "Who could be bored in this house?" And his friend Eusebius replied, "No one who has learned to live with himself."

"You do remember Danny?"

Yes. Oh yes. He was one of those I did so truly love. That whole time is gone now, isn't it? A quark in the fabric of our life.

Another student introduced me to Danny, as I recall. That seems an age ago. Danny had just decided to stop studying for the priesthood, as his Irish father and Italian mother always wished him to. Was searching for a place to go. He was beautifully open. He thought it would be wonderful to know the great and tangled literature of this nation, and to teach.

He came here as a junior. He was not in writing but was in the Issues course. His senior year I was coach of the "College Bowl" team and took that earnest bunch of kids to New York. Danny was the captain. We lost real bad, had a terrible day of it, but he kept us all together, he showed

135

some cool. He was a fraternity boy then, big two-hundred-pounder, had such enthusiasm.

Thinking of Danny makes me think of Bill Brooks too, of when he came bursting in on me. That was some years later, wasn't it, old Chips?

I was dozing over the first batch of papers from the summer writing class when I heard him clomp up the steps and ask the secretary for me. He said "Doctor" before my name and I thought, oh my God, what now? Then he came in, big and tall and smiling, like an ungainly puppy, and I rose to nod and shake his hand and smile back at him quizzically, the very caricature of the tired, irrelevant professor.

Boots, jeans, open shirt, a motorcycle helmet in his hand. Brown and dark-haired, like some ideal young Indian. His smile, the light in his eyes, were beautiful.

"Well, Doc," he said, "well now. I've been meaning to come by to see you ever since I got back. I really need your help, Doc. Good Dave says you're the guy. I know you're going to be a lot of help to me."

Kept calling me "Doc." I managed to get him into a chair, and I sat, and he sat grinning at me happily.

Not one of ours. Older, in his early twenties. Jeans bright, new, motorcycle helmet in red and blue. Just bought his bike, was trying to learn to ride it. Almost fallen off it coming over. Thought he'd come here with what he'd learned, figuring one place was just as good as any other.

"Yes," I said, "I've always thought that—"

"Sure, Doc!" he said.

Where he'd come from was Peru. Two years in the Peace Corps there, building houses, trying to be agricultural advisor to the poor proud Indians there. But they would not learn, they would not learn. So proud, polite, and pitiful— they would not prune, Doc. They would not prune the branches of the little apple trees he planted for them on the mountainside. Jesus, Doc, that was a lonely time—but he had loved those people.

They treated him with courtesy, yet as a strange contagious outsider. So that when he'd met the daughter of an American official and she'd asked him in from the bush to her house and given him an ice-cold Pabst and a kiss, he'd gone back to his shack and cried.

"Oh, it wasn't the kiss, Doc," Bill said. "It was the Pabst!"

Now he wanted to straighten out the vibrations between the people here, which were so bad. He told me then the theory of the eyes.

Penny Reichert was hanging around that day and saw him, the green-eyed girl he married. Oh yes, Bill made it, he's an anthropologist now. He took his bike to Taos, falling off and breaking his leg along the way. He got beat up pretty bad out there by cowboys, but he made it, he was one who made it.

That day Penny had for me another example of her endless unformed prose, the repeated childhood story about old Ben and the big uncatchable bass and her grandfather and his dog.

"Who was that?" she said.

"Who?"

"That guy. God," she said, "he's beautiful."

And that reminds me, also, of my two young writers who married while in school, George and Carmen. That was about the same time, I think. Married out at his home in Abilene.

"It was weird, man," George said. "They hated my hair, man. All my musician buddies got off and came to the wedding, man, a real bunch of freaks. You know? It really freaked out the parents, man. Like, Buffalo Bill just kept arriving on the scene. The only one it didn't bother was my grandma. She was just happy to meet 'George's friends.' Like, she could remember, man, when *her* father looked like that, going out to Abilene."

"But Danny McBride? It was Danny I was asking about."

Yes. But I was going to say something, about the theory of the eyes. Something Bill Brooks told me back then.

"Listen, Doc," he said. "It happens. I mean, every day. This morning. I get up and walk over to the plaza. It's real early and everything is opening up. There's a cop on the corner waiting to cross the kids. I smile and wave to him. He doesn't respond—he looks at me—but it gives him something to think about. It's like when people used to wave to a policeman, smile at them. And he looks like an okay guy, he's decided the best way he can make it is as a policeman. So I meet Good Dave and he has on his bell-bottoms and striped shirt and the beaded band around that truly great head of hair, and his beard is all red and gold in the morning light. So we go into Andy's for a bite of breakfast.

"Well, you know Andy's. It is a fairly honky place. Good Dave doesn't eat there usually. So the waitress comes and gives us the big oblique look, just like in a *movie,* Doc. And I look at her, you know, and realize that that is where she's learned her moves from, and her thoughts. So I look again, and see that she's a skinny woman, middle-aged, who probably lives fifteen miles off somewhere and has to get up and come in here to work, and the sleep is still in her eyes, and she's still tired from the day before. And her eyes, Doc— her *eyes.* They won't look at you. She's looking away from my beads, I see, and from Dave's headband, and his hair. So I sit and wait and look at her until she looks at me. Now, she can hate me now, in this moment—decide I'm a punk or a lech or putting her on—or she can just be a person, the person that she is all inside, Doc, the person that she is anyway, that no one ever *sees*. Like we all are, Doc. I smile at her and I mean it, and she knows it. People know it, Doc. And Dave, who is a lovely guy—he says you remember when he tried to make it in the seminary, Doc, sitting in class barefoot—he smiles at her.

"She doesn't smile then, but just takes our order. So here she is, going back and forth taking orders, snapping answers at people in the booths, slapping down the food and the coffee and the checks, but pretty soon she comes over and pours us some more coffee. 'Thank you,' I say, which isn't much, but I look at her, like, you know, Doc, 'Hello, I realize you are a person, and I know that and it's more important to me than this thing of your *happening* to be our waitress now and I wish, I really wish, that we could talk about something sometime.' You know what I mean, Doc.

"So then she brings the check and puts it down really *gently*. And she really looks at us. Her eyes are kind of smoky-gray, and when they're open like that and not all slitted up they are as pretty as she ever was. And Good Dave gets up and says to her, 'Have a good day,' and smiles and means it, means just that, and Doc, I mean she smiles back.

"'Thank you,' she says to us.

"That's just an example, Doc," Bill said. "Your whole day, every day, everyone's, can go like that."

"Danny McBride went to Vietnam, didn't he, and had a bad experience there? That was why I asked."

Yes. You see, his whole interest studying here became America, its literature, its ideas, its hopes for man. Then he was doing well in a Ph.D. program in the Midwest when they drafted him, had found his lovely dancer girl. I could not imagine him in Canada, exiled from all he loved, his in-

139

terests. So counselled him against Canada. Yes, did so. Took that deep dip into the life of another. Saying to myself the worst thing that could happen was that he be sent to Vietnam. And so of course it happened. To this boy, denied his c.o. status which we thought surely he would get, who had studied most of his young years to be a priest . . .

"It happened to many others."

Yes. Sure. But that's history, sociology. You will forgive me, but I'm speaking only of Danny McBride. He didn't even fight, you know. He deserted, for a day, when he was supposed to go and fight. Wandered around the camp all day until he came upon an old colonel who saw his college ring and learned he could write and type and got him re-assigned. You might say that was lucky. But it was the very system that crushed him. From the first. He wrote when he first got there, from Saigon:

"My first trip beyond the post I experienced people flood. Two, three, four abreast they buzzed by with three, four small people on the humming bikes, flooding me along in the puttering, chain-driven flow. But these mechanized drones did not disturb me as much as the huge O.D. monsters, the olive-drab distortions of our own economy, mammoth trucks bearing the numbers and symbols of the U.S. or RVN, lumbering down the narrow streets.

"The trash, the garbage, the waste is everywhere, in some places piled high as if it were a monument to the strangling population.

"We have smothered this city and this country beyond life. The water buffalo stands staring at the Esso Station with exhaust-reddened eyes, wondering where his pasture has gone. This is insanity, this marching, driving, shouting, screaming, shooting world. It's getting to me. The effects of a complete lack of beauty. Nothing is here to move one's sensibilities. No one is concerned about how one's feelings are affected. This whole bit has to be savage to sustain itself. From the toddling moments of viewing *West Point,* America is taught that there is some warmth of comradeship in our common efforts of imposition upon other peoples. There is none. The ferocity extends to the very core of the organization."

About the same time, and this is strange—or maybe a little later, the Mariner's mind fuzzes a little—my daughter, who loved Danny too, was fourteen and into Love and one Sunday then I took her to the park. There we found a Vanity Fair, the other side of what Danny McBride was going through.

My daughter wandered off and found someone to toss a frisbee with. I was to pretend I didn't know her, should we chance to meet on the path to the popsicle vendor. She disapproved of my khakis and tennis shoes. I was, I told her, posing as a narc.

Rock bands played, plugged in, amplified. A multitude threw frisbees, up and down the slopes, in the streets. All around the park the side shows: yoga, folk singing, rapping, theater extempore. I had my book, *The Rise and Fall of the Third Reich,* and it was odd to sit there reading of how the Hitler youth was formed and controlled, hearing the music, seeing the people swaying to it. Then I looked and saw I was the only one in the park reading.

A guy came and sat by me and I turned to smile and be friendly, and he smiled and was friendly, and I saw he had a *python* coiled in his arms. It scared me.

By me kids sat and did Oms. *Om—Haddee—Haddee Haddee Om—*

I saw a former student named Peter. He was the brightest kid I'd ever had in freshman English. He had gone a long way off, to California and Lucy-in-the-Sky-with-Diamonds, and then come back. He came to sit with me, and looking at me his eyes were terribly clear, like unflawed crystal. Look-

141

ing into those eyes I realized Peter knew things, knew them in ways, I would never know. I asked if he wrote anything anymore. He smiled at the old word freak.

"You'll have to come by sometime," I said, "and talk."

"We're talking now," he said.

But it was Danny whom you asked about, wasn't it?

Danny came home. Weighing just over a hundred pounds he came back, discharged. He had gone completely into himself. Finally he came by our house. He sat with us and stared around the room, as if he did not know this place or us, as if he could not trust us. Could not trust us. Christ! I tried to get him to write about it. Then he went away again. Finally a postcard came from Sweden. And that was also, now, years ago.

"Have you heard from him, then, recently?"

Yes. He came back once again after that. Just before his mother died. He had nearly died on drugs in Sweden. A farmer found him in his field. That family cared for him. Then he found, went into—some kind of place. A way of living, a set of teachings. He embraced it totally, as he would have the priesthood, I suppose. Before he went back I urged him to write to me.

"Did he?"

Yes, once. And that just after he returned to Sweden.

He wrote: "Coming back, I did not feel I hated America, its beauty, its abundance, its searching, its frustration. I think the insanity is inherent in mankind, or else I remain insane. But given that, I have not given up hope in America, though I do not want to be there now. The war ending, I found comfort to be the major force now in America. That is odd, as you would say, isn't it, to have comfort as the goal in life?

"No, I haven't given up hope. But I believe that the situa-

142

tion is worsening, that materialism—regard for matter and not for the spirit of man—grows stronger, that unless America begins to make some real changes our culture will decay spiritually to the point of technological and abstract rule."

And that's the last I heard from him. And that has also been some time now.

"So you don't really know what's happened to Danny McBride?"

No. I have been trying to say I don't. I have a certain faith, you might call it a needful faith, that Danny is all right.

I did see Good Dave the other night, out at the airport. He drives a taxi now. Still wears a headband. He says he has made peace. He works nights, keeps the kids while his wife works days.

Elegy

1. November Noon

THAT day dawned drear and dismal, but the weather was clearing. It did not look like it would rain.

My wife took some hot chocolate in to our daughter. She was six and was going to stay home from school today with a strep throat. I stood in front of the old black-and-white TV in my undershorts with a cup of coffee in my hand. I did not have a class till ten. I saw him come in to the breakfast at the Fort Worth Chamber of Commerce and sit there, without her, and smile. He had style. He refused to wear the hat. She came in. She had style and grace.

"Do you want the car today?" said my wife.

"No. I'll walk."

I walked the mile over to the campus muffled up because I had a sore throat myself. I walked lost in my thoughts and hardly saw anything I walked by. I was going to teach my class of freshmen James Baldwin's essay "Stranger in the Village." Then I would go home and take a nap.

In my office just before class I read the editorial in the *Dallas Times Herald* of the evening before. "The eyes of the world," it said, "also follow the President of the United States, at home and abroad. The eyes of the world are following him to Dallas. We believe both the world and John F. Kennedy will like what is seen here."

At the back of the paper was an ad for Rev. J. C. Hibbard's Water Baptismal Service and an ad for Rev. Billy James Hargis's service at the Polk Street Baptist Church. The sermon was to be "America, Back to God and Americanism."

Sometime before noon I went home and ate a chili dog my wife fixed me. I decided not to have a beer. I was drowsy enough already. Maybe I would really have to take that nap.

I went into the bedroom and sat on a wobbly three-legged stool and watched the President's arrival in Dallas. My daughter was on the bed playing with cut-out dolls. When the President and his lady got in the car to leave Love Field I got up and went into the living room and flopped on the couch and began to read a column in the *New Yorker* about television called "The Air." I was waiting to see JFK at the luncheon in the Trade Mart, wondering what he would say to this Dallas audience, here in this essentially Republican city which was in danger of losing its commercial airport and which had lost the hoped-for Federal Center. I heard my wife call something, a question. My daughter, on the bed, paying closer attention to the TV, told her: "They've shot somebody."

My wife called out again. "Something has happened," she said.

I got up, stood stupidly. Then ran, stumbled into the bedroom.

"Kennedy's been shot," said my little girl.

I collapsed down upon the stool. I said something, I hardly knew what I said. Then I heard myself sobbing. My daughter, affected by my breakdown, began to cry. My wife went to her. I went to stand in the living room. Then I walked outside, breathing deeply. Now the sun shone brightly. The sun stood just a little past where it would be if it were noon.

146

Back in the house I stood and watched the television once

more, to confirm that he was dead. The set was tuned in to the luncheon at the Trade Mart. Everyone had been waiting there. Now they sat or moved around in the black-and-white picture as if they were still waiting. Some of them had started eating. I saw city figures I recognized getting up and down and moving around the rows of tables and talking to people and shaking hands. I saw one of our university people get up and wander around, then stop to look at the table decorations. Each table was decorated with long-stemmed Texas roses and a holder with small replicas of the six flags that had flown over Texas. The TV panned the hall. The mayor and some others stood in a corner in a huddle, like a losing football team.

I told my wife I would go over to the university. She asked if I thought it was dangerous. Maybe I should stay home. No, I said. This was the isolated act of a fanatic. They must be after him.

Walking back to school I saw every mote of sunlight on every tree leaf, every sidewalk crack etched sharply, every crack of paint on the houses that I passed.

On campus I came to the administration building. A small band of people was gathered there. They stood looking at the flag on the nearby flagpole.

"Shouldn't we take it down?" someone said.

"Lower it, you mean," said the p.r. director.

I went into my building, up the stairs to the department offices. Our chairman sat in the outer office where the secretary usually sat. He looked so calm that I burst out, "Haven't you heard? The President is dead—"

"I know," he said. He looked at me as if he wondered if I did not have papers to mark, some grades to record.

In my office my officemate, a man who had just come that year from the East, sat with the telephone in his hands. His wife was shouting into it in fear and terror that they must move away from here.

Back home, my wife told me what she'd heard. She had heard that some schoolchildren had cheered when the announcement was made. We agreed that we were bound to hear a lot of things, that we could not give in to rumor or be frightened. I went to see how my daughter was.

Then I sat with my wife to watch the television. She had moved it into the living room.

It was very strange, sitting in our house in Dallas. The networks had pre-empted the local Dallas stations. We sat in our living room in Dallas and watched the national coverage on TV.

2. Poem

HE *took a twelve-dollar gun*
Carcano (cheese?)
And raised it into new-brilliant sun
The rain had stopped we were bubbleless
(Now it would take God's biggest plastic bubble)
God it was a pretty day
And yet if

Which goes to show
what poets can do
with their correlatives

The shots rang   shock and pain
We were numb   half-dead too
The shock   Why do we have these damn fanatics here?
The grief   anguish   shame
Numbed
But did the children cheer?

The sun warmed the snake and stirred it
Oh Big D little a double l asss
Me no questions I'll tell you no lies

What to do, boys? What we gonna do?
Why, pray We all prayed, didn't we? Biggest
Baptist biggest Methodist   biggest Presby—
The Catholics too   And Jews they know of this
Why pray, boys   then forget   roll up your sleeves
and
Build Dallas!

Blithe spirit to restore!   Dallas don't we love
You   Back to normalcy
(The spirit of W. G. Harding or was it Coolidge
Clapped politely off the stage)

Yes Skyscrapers   some slums too   But he was
Left not right   Of course not right at all
Off his head a lone— Don't say guilt, boys

Okay   He'd (don't say the name, say he) want us to
Go forward
Cheerleaders, three times the scared I mean sacred seven
Waving pom-poms of blood

Well, get the bastard a lawyer anyway   He don't
want a lawyer   Hi, Jack   you covering for
the Jewish press?   Ha ha   Why Jack you
Son of a bitch   like well   I'll be damned
They knew old Jack flawed ruby in our navel
No harm in him
He'd hung around

Good words were said   we have a heavy heart
Yes   (What is the matter, my Lord?)
Like a guest into our home   So welcome
Why we were empowered for
Citizens' arrest   By God I think I'll arrest old—
He'd better watch himself!

Well it could have happened anywhere
There's a Dallas Nevada and a Dallas this and a Dallas
Heaven and a Dallas Hell   Dallas is
everyone   So Big D little a big d little
Hester had her scarlet A

Pray and then forget   We don't want a monument
Let's call a moratorium
on it all   for our hearts are heavy and
The policeman's widow will have enough
Anyway it was Castro   The Mafia did it you know that
Gray pearl ruby hat is the mark—

Oh God!

Hester lived a good life after
Yet it did happen
Oh God
It happened here.

3. *Elegos*

IT is Sunday morning. Twenty years after.

Thus reads the inscription at the memorial at Main and Record:

The joy and excitement of
John Fitzgerald Kennedy's life belonged to all men.

So did the pain and sorrow of his death.

When he died on November 22, 1963, shock and
agony touched human conscience throughout the world.
In Dallas, Texas, there was a special sorrow.

Inside the memorial is the black marble low-lying slab, with "John Fitzgerald Kennedy" marked on it on two sides in gold.

This day, in front of the marker, there is one spray of flowers, with long green stems and a bit of fern: red roses, white and pink camellias. It is from a flower shop in Dallas. The empty envelope is marked "Mr. President."

Now a young couple with two towheaded boys comes in. One boy climbs on the marker, astraddle it. "No," the parents say.

"He's dead, isn't he?" the boy calls back.

A woman with a convention label on her sweater comes in. She kneels, but not to pray, it seems. She reads the envelope on the flowers, quickly leaves.

A family with a girl in a leg cast and two sons comes in. "Who was he?" the smallest asks.

Outside, I look at the words carved in black, hear footsteps slowly going in. A nun enters. She is soon gone, as if she walked right through. A man passes by me, in sweater and jeans, with a canvas bag, just off a bus perhaps. He looks down at the lettering as if he does not know what the marker is at all.

The memorial outside is four hanging walls, an envelope

suspended in space. Inside, it is like being within four shields which keep you from the realities without. Even on this Sunday there are human sounds, of cars, buses, trucks, jets high overhead. But in the memorial there is only muffled sound, and the footsteps of those who enter.

One hundred yards west is the grotesque old courthouse, an individualistic building of red and gray stone, turreted. Just across the street then, Dealey Plaza, "birthplace of Dallas." Beyond, the grassy knoll known to all the world.

It is church-time now in Dallas. Many people are now in church in Dallas. (As many are not.) There are only a few at the plaza, near the knoll, by the famous building. The flat prose of the Dealey Plaza plaque says: "President Kennedy expired at Parkland Memorial Hospital at 1:00 P.M." There are two roses there, placed on a hedge. They look like they came from the same spray as those in the memorial.

Now a woman approaches, holding other flowers. She places them there, kneels, prays. I see that her flowers are artificial, red and yellow plastic flowers with shiny leaves. They will last, perhaps she thinks, they will last.

Now it is noon, as it was that day so many years ago. Now my daughter who called out to us that day is grown and my younger girl hardly knows this story. Now I must be going.

I stop and say a brief prayer of wonder, for his life and yours and mine, for all the joy and insanity of it, the grief and love, the purpose that eludes us. I ask forgiveness for my part in it, all the sins of omission and commission.

Then I drive back up Main Street. Most of Dallas will be home soon, waiting for the Cowboy game to come on television.

About the Author

Marshall Terry is professor of English and director of the Creative Writing Program at Southern Methodist University, where he has taught since 1954. He is author of three novels, *Old Liberty, Tom Northway,* and *Ringer,* and of short fiction, essays, and book reviews. His novel *Tom Northway* was co-winner of the Jesse H. Jones Award of the Texas Institute of Letters in 1968, and his short story, "The Antichrist," was named best of the year by that organization in 1972.

Photo by Joe Mark Horn

Typesetting by G&S, Austin, Texas
Printing and binding by Thomson-Shore, Dexter, Michigan
Design and production by Whitehead & Whitehead, Austin, Texas